*For my three favorite creative artists*
*Kerry, Gus and Henry*

# On Top Of Everything

by

Neal Zagarella

# This Works Press

## Ipswich MA

thisworkspress@gmail.com

This is a work of fiction. Any resemblance to actual persons, living or dead, events, or locales is entirely coincidental.

ISBN: 978-1-312-4491-4

The chapter, "Boom", was originally published in *Madmen of Lynn* by Ring of Bone Press

# On

# Top

# of

# Everything

# FIRST

I'm walking down Carter Street on my way over to get Burke and Rosie. This is my life before cars and exploration and the great American night. We're pre-drivers, teenage drifters, loosed nightly from our parents' grip to roam the dark mysteries of our neighborhood streets. It is the heat of an early June evening and Burke, Rosie and I are going to meet Tommy and his brother George for our first night of drinking. After much negotiation, cajoling, and promising we finally convinced George to buy us our first beers, mainly with an idle threat that we would tell his parents all the shit we knew he did behind their backs.

"Alright, alright," he said, seeing he was cornered. "But I'm going to be there with you. You need someone to teach you these things." George the teacher. Somehow I can't see him at the front of a classroom.

I lope down Carter and across Winthrop, the big main road that separates me and Tom's neighborhood from Burke and Rosie's. Striding along, it's like I'm carrying a roll of loot or some sacred secret. This is a new big boy adventure, as scary and exciting as girls. I'm just fourteen, still really a little kid, but standing in the doorway of the great unknown, the big world of beer, girls, cars. Tonight I'll take my first step inside.

Striding up Elm Street, I see Burke in his usual place, hanging around Ant's driveway, basically doing nothing but watching Ant perpetually fixing his black Mustang.

Burke is sixteen, the oldest and tallest in our group, and Ant is his hero. Ant got his name because he didn't grow for a long time, but at age 16 he shot up to about 5'11 and filled out a little bit and there is now nothing particularly anty about him, except his nickname. He just graduated high school at the beginning of June and when he's not working on his own car, he's usually working downtown at Sully's Garage fixing other people's junk jalopies.

I walk up to the driveway and exchange upward chin nods with Burke. We're so cool we don't even have to talk to say hello. Ant is under the car working on some aspect of the engine, with some name that I can't recognize or define.

"Tonight's the night," I say to Burkie.

"Really Pete? You really think Georgie Jerkoff will come through?" he asks.

"George'll come through," I answer, though I'm not sure he will. Anything with George seems risky. None of us trust him. "Hey, why've ya never asked Ant to buy for us? He's old enough now."

"His father's a cop, dipshit," Burke reprimands.

"Yeah, and you're a dipshit, hee hee," I hear from under the car. Ant I do trust, to give me shit. It's a pretty good guess that he won't be buying for us anytime soon.

Coming down the street now, cutting through the early evening summer heat, is a girl, blond, in a skirt and a frilly-like top and some blocky-heeled shoes that lift her up and that she shouldn't be wearing on the bumpy, cracked sidewalks around here.

Girl is not an accurate term for what is moving toward us here. I know girls. This is like a woman coming, with the sun dusking low behind her, and the closer she gets the more jiggly her top gets and the wider her hips swing, like a pendulum on some giant clock swinging, striking real thing, striking good-bye little boy days, striking fever in our chests. The more she sways, the closer she comes, the wider Burkie and me's jaws hang open, our eyes fixated on that pendulum swing hypnotist watch, hip notice.

Without a word to us she makes a fist with her knuckles and tap, tap, taps on the fender of Ant's Mustang. Ant rolls halfway out from under the car and grins up between the girl's legs.

"Nice view, but stop the banging on my fender"

"Stop the banging?" She smiles wickedly, angelic. Me and Burkie, breathless. "You sure about that?"

"I'm almost done here," Ant says.

"Be done and ready in an hour," the girl says and walks back up the street, so cool, like she has three more boyfriends' driveways to stop at.

Ant slides back under the car and me and Burkie watch her walk off the way she came, her ass penduluming down the road, the rhythm of her swaying off into the setting sun, like the details of a dream dissolving in the first few moments of morning. After some distance we come to and exhale.

"Be ready in an hour, Ant," I say in my best bitchy girl's voice, all high and shrill. Now I'm the shitgiver. "Boy, are you pussy whipped."

"Fuck you, Pete. You don't even know what a pussy looks like," Ant cracks from beneath the car. He rolls his head out from under the engine so I can see him grinning upwards at us and continues his jabbing. "If a pussy stole something from you and you went down to the police station to identify it in the line up, you'd be able to pick out the pussy because it would be the one thing in the lineup you'd never seen before."

Burkie almost falls over cracking up, his first sounds and movement since the girl appeared and then disappeared. "The one thing you never saw!" he cackles.

Burkie and I leave Ant's and lank our way down the road toward Rosie's. Rosie is really Bobby O'Leary, but somehow we found out that his middle name is Roseland, his mother's maiden name, and decided to be assholes about it. By right, he should be Bobby O, or Big O or something. Not with us around.

"That chick was amazing," I marvel, more to myself than toward Burkie.

"Yeah, you know it. That's Ant. He's magic. He's always getting chicks like that." Burkie's worshiping his hero, as usual, but I have to admit that Ant always seems to have pretty girlfriends, and tonight's beauty might top them all.

"His sister's magic, too," I add. "I wouldn't throw her outta bed for eating crackers." Ant has an older sister Colleen, long, brown hair, gorgeous. Neighborhood legend.

"What do you know about having a girl in bed?" Burkie asks.

Nothing, of course, I admit only to myself.

"First of all, Colleen would laugh at you. Second of all, Ant would beat the shit out of you. Anyway, right now I'm concentrating on somebody else's sister," Burke says.

We get to Rosie's and rap on his door. The sister of Burkie's thoughts, Karen O'Leary, comes rushing up, springs open the door and looks up at my friend.

"Hi, Burke. What's up?" she smiles upward.

"Not much. You girls gonna be around later if we come looking for you?" Burkie asks. He runs a hand through his blond bangs and lets them fall back down over his forehead.

"Nope. Babysitting," she turns dour. "So you can hang out with my stupid brother."

"Need any help with that?" Burke flirts.

"You mean with babysitting?" Karen returns.

"Maybe," answers Burke, with arched eyebrows.

"Maybe," Karen tosses back over her shoulder as she turns away with a little twist of her backside.

"Good Karen, and you?" I say to no effect. She is only thirteen, but her breasts got promoted a couple grades ahead. One day she was Rosie's little kid pain in the ass sister, and the next she was keeping us all up nights lying in our beds in the gloaming darkness, sleepless in balls of anguish and sweat.

"I'll be right down, guys," Rosie yells from his upstairs bedroom.

"Take your time," says Burke, keeping his eyes trailing after Karen. He's content to stay around here and flirt, lay the groundwork for something later, turn his midnight dreams into reality. I, too, am in no hurry. I have my own reason to stall.

"Hey Karen," I ask. "How come it's always you babysitting and not Rosie?"

"'Cos my stupid mother hates me."

"You're stupid," pipes Rosie, entering the room.

"Shut up, Bobby."

"You shut up, and if that pukebag Serino calls, tell him I'm gonna throw him off the Merrick Street train bridge."

Burke perks up. "Who's Serino?

"Tony Serino. He's in my Spanish class. He likes me," Karen curlicues.

"He wants to rape her," Rosie asserts. "And my little tramp sister is willing."

"Shut up, Rosie," Karen retorts, tarting up the syllables of Rosie.

"Have fun babysitting," Rosie finishes and leads us out the door.


I walk slowly as we move back down the road. We have to go past Ant's house again to meet Tommy and his brother George. I drag along at a molasses pace.

"C'mon Pete, what are you asleep?" Burke chides. I don't think he's really pissed at me. He's probably thinking about this Serino kid, maybe calling little busty Karen and spoiling his own plan. I bet he'd grab an end and help Rosie toss the kid off a bridge.

"Let's take our time, Burkie. That chick's gonna be comin' back to Ant's house. Remember?"

"Oh now I get it."

"What chick? Rosie asks.

Burkie points to the horizon where like some hallucination, she reappears moving, floating hypnotically, dreamlike from some distant memory or movie shot, slowly, swayingly, forward into our view, our reality, the girl. The Woman. Blonde hair, jiggly, frilly top, hips swaying rhythmically ever forward, toward us. Her mouth, as it sharpens into sight, lips slightly upturned in a knowingness. Some mystery behind those lips, that mouth. She knows things, answers. I don't even know the questions.

She comes. I fall asleep in a gaze at her entirety. Hips, lips, eyes now, pale, walking directly toward me. Rosie and Burke somehow summon the ability to move about or speak to each other or some such thing. I don't know. I'm entranced. She is coming directly toward me. I smell lilacs. She's inches away. Her lips part.

"Hey little shit," she purrs, placing her hand on top of my head. She leans in and down, she's an inch or two taller than me, and softly presses her lips flush against mine. "It's not polite to stare."

She brushes past me and up Ant's driveway toward his door, full sway and careless. The softness of her lips, the lilacy smell of her, stays with me.

Some impulse overtakes me and I burst into a run of about fifteen steps down the road. The boys explode into cacophonous laughter.

"What are you afraid of, Pete?" Burkie sputters. "Its just a girl."

"Yeah, now you're in a hurry," Rosie shouts after me.

"Goin' home to jerk off, Pete?"

"Yeah, is your peter hard Peter?"

13

"You're just jealous," I bark back, but I don't care much about the catcalls and jokes. I have been kissed by a pretty girl, an almost woman. Kissed!

"You act like you've never been kissed before," Rosie says. I have never been kissed before.

"I've been kissed plenty of times."

"Your mother doesn't count," Burkie grins.

"Oh shut the fuck up. You all wish she kissed you."

"She was making fun of you," Rosie says.

"Yeah, if she kissed me," Burkie brags, "We'd still be kissing."

"Well, she didn't kiss you. She kissed me."

"Alright, alright," Burke says, "Tell us all about your half-second kiss. Did you get hard?"

"Her lips," I start, searching for the right words, "Were like flowers."

More uproarious laughter. Burkie waps the back of my head and says, "Come on loverboy, let's go get drunk."


We're sitting on the rock wall down at the end of Clifton Street by the old abandoned factory waiting for Tommy and his big brother George to come with the beer and open the door to the new world. This is what Christopher Columbus must have felt like, or Magellan.

"He's not gonna show," Burke complains.

"Why wouldn't he show?" I ask, trying to be optimistic.

"Cos we already gav'em the money," says Rosie. Why did we ever trust George? That's the question we're all asking.

"I'm gonna kick Tommy's ass," Burke declares.

"It's not Tommy's fault," reminds Rosie. "It's fuckin' George. We should have never trusted him."

"Yuh," Burke resigns. "They're not gonna show."

They show. George's beat up blue Chevy Impala, a real boat, glides into view, slowing in front of us, Tommy smiling like King Shit in the passenger seat, like he bought the beer himself, and George pulling to the side of the road and parking.

George gets out and walks toward us, his hands full with straws and a jar of peanut butter. Tommy comes behind him, grinning with the twelve pack of Miller High Life beer dangling from his right hand.

"How we gonna divide this up," Rosie asks.

"Everybody take a straw," George commands. "You all get two. I get four. That's my tip. The peanut butter's for your breath later."

None of us question anything. We're all afraid to drink and afraid to let that fear show. At least that's what I feel. But no one wants to piss off George and have him take the beer back and close the door to that great mystery adult world that stands just before us golden in this June heat.

One by one we twist off the caps and dip our straws in the bottles. Hesitantly, I suck up some yellow liquid through the straw and shudder involuntarily. I quick check around to see if the other guys saw my little fit. They couldn't have or there would be screams of laughter.

"You okay Little Peter?" George chuckles. He's always got what we call a shiteating grin on his face.

"Yuh, this is good," I lie.

"Why the straws?" Burkie asks.

"It multiplies the affects," Rosie says.

"What do you know about it?" George prods, pointing a pudgy finger at Rosie.

"Plenty," Rosie answers.

Tommy's sucking down the beer like its soda. He's shorter than his brother George, but he has the kind of long black hair parted in the middle that girls like. "George, can I get a third one if I finish first?"

George looks over to me and my nearly full bottle and says "Maybe you can have Little Peter's second one. I don't think he's gonna make it through the first."

Burke pipes up, "Don't worry about loverboy. He's just a little shooken up."

"Yeah, its hard to drink and cum at the same time," Rosie grins.

"What's this?" Tommy turns to me.

"Nothin'," I answer. I want to talk, talk, talk about it, but I know the kinda shit that's going to come my way. Really, I'd like to just be alone, so I could memorize the lips, the girl, the kiss.

"Oh c'mon," Burkie revs. "You stole Ant's girlfriend from him."

George laughs loudly, "That blonde? Jenny? You wouldn't know what to do with her."

"She kissed me."

Screams of laughter.

"She kissed you?" George doubts, his grin springing open wide like one of those carnival game clown mouths you shoot water into with fake pistols. "She wouldn't touch you, and you wouldn't know what the fuck to do with her."

"She kissed me," I say and take a long tug on my beer, twitching only slightly, until it gurgles. "She kissed me on the lips and I'm ready for my second beer."

When we've each forced down two beers George takes the remainder of the twelve pack and saunters to his car. Getting in he says, "If any of you get caught, it wasn't me that bought it for you. Tommy, take the peanut butter. It's the best shit to get the beer smell off your breath. Petey," he points a stubby finger towards me, "I'll beat the shit out of you if you get caught."

"I'm not gonna get caught," I pout. It's always me he threatens. I'm the smallest kid. He doesn't try that with Burkie or Rosie because they'd probably be able to take him.

We pass around the jar, each plopping a fat finger full of the peanut butter in our mouths. It tastes way better than the beer. Tommy crams the jar in his back pocket and promises George, "No one's gonna get caught."

Off George rolls in his big blue boat, and we go walking down the path that leads through some woods and then out to the giant Whyte Fuel tank. My head's a little fuzzy and my tongue feels rubbery and thick.

It is decided now, with our two beer buzz, that we are going to climb the metal steps that wind up around the big tank and get on top of it. I'm scared shitless of heights and of getting picked on. My legs feel longer and looser than usual under this alcoholy fog. I'm not staggering, but

I do have to concentrate to keep my legs from going Wizard of Oz scarecrow on me.

"You ok?" Rosie asks. We've fallen back a little behind Burke and Tommy.

"Yeah, I'm good. But that beer sucked, didn't it?" I say, finding it a chore to pronounce my consonants.

"Yeah, I bet Budweiser's better."

"I don't think I could ever be an alcoholic. I don't like the taste that much."

"You acquire a taste for it," says Rosie. He knows what he's talking about. His dad gets drunk a lot. He's an alcoholic, I think. When the whole O'Leary family was living together, you could walk by on any night and hear him screaming at Rosie's mom and her screaming back. Things are better over there since the divorce, or at least quieter. Rosie never says it, but I can tell he misses his Dad. He only sees him on Sundays now.

The fuel tank rises above the trees and we stumble out into the clearing. How am I going to get these jelly legs up those winding stairs?

"Come on you drunks," Tommy smiles snidely. "Let's start climbing."

Rosie and I hang back a little bit. "My stomach feels like shit," he says.

Tommy and Burke ignore him and start their climb up the metal fire escape type steps.

"Oh God," Rosie gasps and leans on the tank.

"C'mon you cowards," Tommy yells down as they continue up, up.    Rosie lets out a big roar and a gash of pukes sprays the side of the tank.

"I gotta help Rosie. He's puking," I shout, thrilled to have an excuse to not climb the giant tank.

"Lightweights," Tommy yells down, as he and Burkie cackle and climb.

"You ok Rosie?"

"Yuh. Yuh. Much better." He says wiping his mouth. After a few deep breaths he yells up, "Hey Tommy, you got that peanut butter?"

"Yeah," Tommy shouts back. "Come and get it."

"I'm good now," Rosie says to me. "Lets go up."

Oh shit.

"You sure?" I ask, but Rosie doesn't answer. He just begins climbing and I follow him up, up about ten feet up. There's probably thirty more to go. My chest and head are hot, my legs weak and shaky, jelly. I can't do it. I'm stopped.

"C'mon, it's just walking up stairs," Rosie says. "You do it all the time. Don't look down." The stairs I usually walk up don't have these big spaces you can see through all the way to the ground. Besides, where else am I supposed to look?

I don't say anything, but carefully, slowly, I turn around. Gripping the rod-iron railing tightly, I retrace my steps until I'm back at the bottom, safe again on Earth.

"Oh look," Tommy yells, peering over the edge. He and Burke are now standing on the top. "It's Howard the Coward." He snears and hucks a big hunk of spit down. I scramble backward from the tank not wanting to get rained on by Tommy's loogie. Laughter echoes all around. "Howard the Coward!"

After the boys return to earth, it's decided to head over to Rosie's. His mother's out and his sister is babysitting. "Where's that peanut butter, Tommy?" Rosie asks. Tommy produces it from the back pocket of his jeans.

"Everybody have some, I don't want my sister to smell any alcohol."

"Or puke," Tommy chuckles. We cut back out through the woods and onto Clifton. From there we get back on to my street, Carter, over the big main road and up towards Ant's house on Elm. From there we'll head up to Rosie's.

"I shoulda threw you off that tank," Rosie tells Tom.

"Howard was down there. He could've caught me," Tommy's says with a whack to my shoulder.

"What a view up there," Burke notes. "Downtown Endicott on one side, downtown Taft on the other"

"Yah, you can even see the rides at Vincent Beach."

We'll get you up there one day," Rosie asides to me. Oh, shit, I'm thinking. I have the high place I need. I love being up in my room looking out the window at Carter and Clifton two stories below, or across Winthrop at the rooftops and trees of Burkie and Rosie's neighborhood. That's high enough for me.

"Hey Pete, maybe Ant's girl is waiting to give you another kiss," Burke yucks.

"Yeah, Howard," Tommy chimes in with my new nickname. "Maybe this time she'll let you touch her titties." Everbody's laughing.

"Shut up Tommy. You weren't even there."

"Oh hey," Tommy says as a car rolls past us. It's Ant's gorgeous sister Colleen. "Hey maybe Colleen wants to do you, too."

"Shut up."

She gets out of her car and throws her long brown hair behind her with a whip of her neck. She hears a breathless chorus of Hey Colleens and Hi Colleens.

"Hey boys," she smiles brightly and then casually whips her hair back around and heads up the driveway to the secrecy of her house, her room, and out of our night. We are left goofy on the street lamp sidelines. The mystery life of a beautiful, older girl.

After Colleen is safely inside and we're a couple houses down the street, Rosie takes a poll. "Who would you rather have? Colleen, or Ant's girlfriend?"

"Let's ask the expert," Tommy snides in my direction.

"Oh Christ, I'd be happy with either," I tell the truth.

"But you've had Ant's girl," Tommy says.

"Jenny just kissed me."

"Oh, now it's Jenny. How romantic," trumpets Rosie.

"She was making fun of you, dipshit. For staring at her tits," Burke points.

"It wasn't like that. She kissed me and it was nice."

"Nice? You pissed your pants," Burkie says. "You ran home to your mother."

"You ran?" Tommy pounces.

"Like from a burning building," says Burkie, igniting another explosion of laughter.

"Oh, what a Howard. Peter gets his little peter hard and he needs to go home to Mommy. Did you cream your pants, Howard?"

"You've never even…" I start, then stop.

"Never even what?" Tommy replies.

My words are way ahead of me. Tommy's way ahead of me. During the last school year he had two different girlfriends, and there always seems to be another standing in his line. I know there's not a single 'never even' that I've done that he hasn't. Except one. "Never even kissed an eighteen year old."

"That wasn't a real kiss," Tommy snears.

"Felt real."

"How would you even know what real is?"

"Ant's chick is real," Burke says, coming over to my side.

"She's pretty hot," agrees Rosie.

"Yeah, and she kisses hot," I proudly finish.

"Oh yeah, titstarer," Tommy mocks.

"I wasn't staring at her tits."

"She said you were," Burke blurts, going back over.

"I was staring at her face. She's pretty."

"Oh my God! Howard's in love," Tommy roars,

"She's pretty," I protest. "You guys tell'im."

Rosie backs me, "Oh, she's definitely pretty."

"Pretty much getting split wide open by Ant right about now," Burke shoots.

I don't want to think about that. She has soft lips that she placed on mine softly. And she smells like lilacs. Don't wreck it.

"Oh shit, Howard. She's cheating on you," Tommy wrecks.

"Anyway, I vote for Colleen," says Burke.

"Me, too," says Rosie. "But I'd take either."

I just hunch up my shoulders and keep walking. What can I possibly say here that won't get me a fountain of shit? I wish I were home in my darkness bed, huddled beneath sticky summer sheets, thinking of those lips, that kiss, her face.


We get to Rosie's house and have one more round of peanut butter before we walk in. His sister Karen is watching the Duke's of Hazzard with another neighborhood girl, Linda.

"Where's the kid?" Rosie asks her.

"Who Tony? He's upstairs in my bed," she answers.

"Did he call?"

"No, Dad. Calm down."

"I'm not Dad," Rosie barks.

Burke smiles at the mention of this Serino kid's non-call. He plops himself on the couch next to Karen and begins to chat her up. Rosie goes upstairs to check on his little brother.

Tommy takes the center ring. "Hey girls," he says, gripping me by the collar. "Have you met Howard the Coward here? He's the only one who wouldn't go to the top of the Whyte Fuel tank."

"You went to the top," Karen marvels, keeping her eyes locked on Burkie. They continue their own flirting.

Tommy concentrates on Linda. She's my age, but a school year behind because she stayed back in first grade. She doesn't have Karen's breasts, but she's cute, with long sandy-colored hair, brown eyes and an innocence that keeps her out of our sweaty midnight longings. Somehow she is beyond our dirty dreaming.

"I'll take you to the top sometime, if you wanna go," he offers.

"No way," she replies. "I'm scared of heights."

"There's nothing to be scared of. I'll be with you."

"No way I'm going up there."

"You and Howard," Tommy says, disgusted, almost to himself. He gives me a little push on the chest, which I try to pretend not to feel. Rosie returns and we sit and lean about the place and all fall into watching The Dukes in the stuffy heat of Rosie's living room. The girls eek at Bo and Luke Duke. The boys groan at Daisy and her short shorts, her Daisy Dukes. When the show's over, Linda announces that she is going home.

Karen lifts her head from close conversation with Burke and says, "Why you leaving so early, Lin?"

"Oh, my parents want me home early for some reason tonight. I think we're doing something in the morning."

Karen's half-listening. "Oh. Well, bye," she shrugs, and fully reengages with Burke.

Tommy turns toward Linda and tries to invite himself, "You don't wanna walk home alone, do you?"

"It's not too far," she says, cheerfully.

"I don't mind taking you," Tommy offers.

"I'll be fine," she adds with a bit of pretty, lips together, fourteen year old firmness.

"You're brave. I bet Howard here wouldn't go out by himself," Tommy chuckles, giving up on Linda, returning to his favorite sport.

"Maybe you're right, Tommy," she agrees, but looks at me. "Pete, will you walk me to my house?"

Will I? "Yuh, yes," I stammer, scrambling to my feet. Why does she even know I'm alive?

"Howard? He can't go. Who's going to walk him back?" Tommy questions with an exaggerated laugh.

Karen and Burkie interrupt their flirtation to absently say good-bye.

"Don't do anything I wouldn't do," Rosie offers obligatorily.

"I'll be right back," I say as we leave. It sounds stupid.

I open the door and feel the freshness of the outside air. We enter silently into the warm June night, walking side by side in silence. Me, head down pondering what words to say and having nothing, glancing quickly at Linda looking straight ahead, the side of her face partially obscured by the waterfall of her long blond hair. Her, just walking beside, a miracle. Why did she pick me for this walk? And, what should I do? Tommy or Burkie would know what to do, would know what she was thinking. Anybody else would do something.

"He's stupid," she says suddenly.

"Huh?"

"Tommy's stupid," she repeats, keeping her gaze ahead of her, up the road. "He shouldn't be making fun of you."

"Oh, I don't care. He's alright."

"I care," she says, turning her face toward me for the first time. "He's supposed to be your friend."

"He is my friend."

"He's a jerk, okay? He can't say anything unless he's putting someone on the spot."

"He's nice to you."

"That's not being nice," she corrects.

She's right, I know, and feel a ripple of gladness dance across my chest.

We turn the corner onto Porter Street, and the right on to Ford Street where she lives, falling deeply into silence. My head begins to warm with shame because she feels sorry for me, but under my ribs there is a growing ecstasy blossoming. She cares about me. But, why? How?

This is when some other kid would do something, say something, I think. We walk on, slowly reeling in her house, now just two driveways away. Still, I can't speak.

"You know, Pete," she saves me. "You're the only one who's never made fun of me for staying back."

"Why would I?"

"Everybody else does. Even Karen, and she's like my best friend."

"I won't. Ever," I promise.

"I won't ever make fun of you, either," she says, really looking at me. The warmth in my head is not shame anymore, but something blush colored. The jelly has returned to my legs, but it is not from the beer earlier.

We stand in her driveway. Her Mom fusses about in the glowing kitchen window.

"Do you like grape soda," Linda asks.

"Yeah," I burst.

"Mom," she calls in through the screen. "Can I give Pete a soda? He walked me home."

"Of course, honey."

I stand awkwardly at the door while Linda goes in. Her mother, with the can all ready, hands it to her like a relay baton. Linda opens the can and then the door and hands it to me.

"See you tomorrow," she smiles. My breath catches.

"Thanks," I say. "Bye."

I turn around and walk back down the driveway. I look back to see her in the kitchen light glow of the window, smiling and talking to her Mom. She goes off. To her room, I imagine. Her sandy-colored hair the last of her to leave.

I raise the can of soda to my mouth. It is sweet on my lips, softly sparkling on my tongue. I drink it in full, long tugs as I pad out of her driveway and down the street. A couple houses down, I raise the empty can to the starry summer sky, and break into a full sprint.

# SATURDAY MORNING

Three things become real to me all at the same time. I'm awake. It's Saturday morning. I'm smiling.

Perhaps I've been smiling all night here in my nesty bed. Smile sleeping, smile dreaming.

Last night I lullabied myself to sleep repeating the words me and Linda said to each other on our miracle walk home. I said them over and over, trying to remember them exactly, say them the exact same way we said them to each other.

To each other. What an amazing phrase to be included in when the other is Linda, sandy haired, smiling, soda in hand. That was the movie playing on the big screen of my eyelids last night as I drifted, dreamy, into sleep. Her.

And on top of everything it is Saturday morning and that's usually enough on its own.

There can be no better feeling in the world for a fourteen year old boy like me, than the beginning of a summer Saturday morning, particularly the first Saturday morning of the summer. It is like cresting the slow crawl up a rollercoaster, nearing its very top, knowing the whole thrill of the downward plummet, the exhilarating speed, the loopy twists and turns, is about to begin right dead ahead of you.

But, how would I know that? Only a kidnapper could get me on a rollercoaster. I couldn't even get half way up the tank at Whyte Fuel last night. Burkie and Tommy went right up like it was nothing, a little stroll in the park. Even Rosie pulled it together and climbed to the top with the other guys after he puked his guts out. Me, I staggered back down the steps clinging to the thin rod iron railing, Costello to everybody else's Abbott, scared and stuck to the ground.

But that was last night, before Linda asked me to walk her home.

And now it is Saturday morning. For me, this is like the moment when I first hear the ring of the ice cream truck's bell as it pulls onto my corner of Carter Street. Or better, because the ice cream's better, it's when the pigtailed girl at Chillwell's Creamery slides the hot fudge sundae through the window to me. All that joy right in front of me in a little plastic bowl, plus the pigtailed girl and her freckles always being so nice, like she's happy to see me.

Saturday's are good in winter, too. It is, after all, the beginning of the weekend, hugely important during the school year.

During those months, though, they always arrive with the specter of 9 'o'clock Saturday school, or Sunday school as my mother always, inexplicably, calls it. It drives me crazy. Both my mother's annoying habit and the schooling itself. Each Saturday me and my fellow public school Catholic kids go to the local parish school, St. Mary's, to be educated in religion. They call it catechism class at St. Mary's, which is almost as strange as my mother calling it Sunday school. Catechism sounds like a bug or an internal organ or some kind of big, tropical storm. It's really just the name of the boring textbook they give us to study.

My neighborhood friends, Tommy, Burke and Rosie all attend St. Mary's during the week, so they don't have to suffer this long, dull dripping morning hour, this cruel bite out of their weekend, every single Saturday. It is worse than watching paint dry, because at least there you start out seeing the glistening wet paint. These classes are like staring at already dried paint. So on those Saturday mornings I have to wait until 10 o'clock as I run to my parents' waiting car to feel the thrill of a beautiful Saturday.

I awake this morning with more than the normal amount of Saturday sweetness. Not just Bugs Bunny and Daffy Duck Saturday morning cartoons with there sunny, jingly cold cereal commercials, not just the hours ahead of free time to look at my baseball cards and play my secret sports leagues, not just the day and night ahead to hang out with my friends. More.

Today as I lay drowsing in my Saturday a.m. bed, the morning sun is glowing inside of me. Well, not the sun exactly, something better. Something no one else has or can see. No one else but Linda and me.

Cute, quiet, innocent, brown eyed, long-haired Linda made a promise to me and I to her. Me, little 14 year old boy, trying to be a big kid teenager all night, getting my first taste of alcohol, getting my first kiss from a non-relative, trying and failing to climb the great giant tank of Whyte Fuel, chickening out really, and earning that nickname – Howard the Coward – that Tommy made up for me. All these things happening to me, at me, in me and none of them really mattering at all any more, except the promise. The very first promise to me ever from a girl and my very first to a girl.

And I have no idea what it really means other than it is sacred and solemn and serious and I am going to keep it like I am a safe and it is inside me.

Yesterday morning none of this was possible, but now it is today and it is more than possible, it is real. The last thing Linda said to me last night was "See you tomorrow." She handed me a grape soda and said, "See you tomorrow." And today is tomorrow.

Those Saturday morning "Sunday School" sessions must have had some affect on me because those words 'she handed me a grape soda and said' remind me now of the part of the gospel that goes 'he took the cup, gave it to his disciples and said,' not that I'm comparing Linda to Jesus. I did take the cup, the grape soda, and did drink from it. I don't know about the blood part, but I do hope it is the new and everlasting covenant, as the gospel says.

It's funny, I've heard those words said so many times in church and in catechism class that they are memorized into me. I'm sure I could say them cold even before I knew that covenant was just another word for promise.

Now here I am in bed smiling on Saturday morning. I feel much older and much younger all at the same time, a feeling of newness and wonder expanding inside of me like the universe. Last night I longed for the mysteries of alcohol, older girls and the vast summer night. Today, after kisses from two beer bottles and one beautiful eighteen-year old girl, my head is dizzy about a secret, quiet promise from a girl my age. What do I do with this but hold it? Hold on to it.


I emerge from my room and go downstairs to the family kitchen and pour a bowl of Cheerios, splash in milk and a spoonful of sugar, and offer some customary good mornings to my Mom and Dad. Everything is normal, I pretend. This goes on and on. Silence, except for the chewing and the ruffling of newspaper pages. I'm bursting.

Like a trumpet the phone rings. I leap. It's only 9 o'clock Saturday morning and the phone is ringing in my house. This is her. Could it be her, I wonder, racing to the phone? Stop. Gather.

"Hello," breathless.

"Hello…Pete?" It's not her. It's my friend Tommy. Tommy the climber of fuel tanks, who gave me my Howard the Coward nickname. My best friend since I can remember.

"Where the hell did you go last night?" he whispers through the phone lines. "You didn't get caught did you?"

"Oh, hey Tommy," I deflate. "Why are you whispering?"

"Did you get caught?" And now I realize what he is talking about. Last night's beer, our first ever.

"No, no. Everything is cool."

"Well, why didn't you come back to Rosie's?"

"I didn't feel like it."

"Did you get it on with Linda?" he asks in a voice that implies there is no way I would ever get it on with Linda or anyone else, whatever get it on really means.

"No, we just talked."

"Oh yuh? What did you talk about?"

"Nothing really."

"You were probably pissing your pants."

"Not really, I got kissed by an eighteen year old, had my first beers and walked home another pretty girl. Good night, all in all," I brag.

"Shhh!" Tommy breaks in. "Can your parents hear you?"

"No. No. Everything's cool."

"Well, keep it down anyway. Ten to one you'll get us caught with your big mouth." He doesn't even realize that ten to one is lousy odds. I learned that betting horses in the newspaper with my Dad. No real money involved, just competition and learning about adult things. My Dad doesn't go to the track, but he did when he was a kid, and after he got out of the Navy at the end of World War II. We pick the horses in the newspaper everyday, then check the results the next day to see how we did, or how we would have done if we actually went to the track.

"Alright, alright," I assure him. "Do you wanna shoot some hoops later?" There is a basketball hoop nailed to the telephone poll across from Linda's house. Sometimes if she's home and sees us, she comes out and sits on her front step.

"You afraid to go over to Linda's without me?" Tommy chides.

"I'm not afraid. I was there last night. It's just hard to play one on one hoops with only one," I lie. I can't imagine myself walking over to Ford Street and just knocking on Linda's door.

"Yeah, right. I'll go with you. I gotta mow my lawn first, though. How 'bout after lunch, like one?"

"Sounds good. Come get me around one."

"Sure. Just keep quiet about last night," Tommy warns.

After breakfast I go up to my room and take out my box of baseball cards. I first started collecting them with Tommy in 1969 when I was 6. My Dad would bring me home one nickel pack a day with 5 cards and a big pink piece of bubble gum. A couple years later I was feeling older and wanted to please my mother and I threw them all away, about two thousand of them, from those first '69's right up through 1973. I only saved two, Luis Aparicio, my idol, the basestealing phenom shortstop of The Chicago White Sox and later my Boston Red Sox, and Harmon Killebrew, with his mammoth Popeye forearms. Who wouldn't love a home run hitter with a name like that?

To show you what a good guy Tommy is, being a year older he'd always have more cards than me, but every time I got a card in a pack that I already had, he would trade me one I didn't have for it. Even though he didn't need that card. Later on when his parents' were getting on his back about his baseball cards, he just gave them all to me. Of course, all those cards went, too, when I threw them all out.

In 1975, the Red Sox got really good with two rookies, Fred Lynn and Jim Rice, and I started in collecting again. I've got a box of about fifteen hundred from then to now, including a couple hundred new 1977's. I especially like getting cards of the old stars from my first real summer of awareness, guys like Killebrew, Brooks Robinson, Tom Seaver and, of course, Boston's own Carl Yastrzemski. The really legendary ones like Willie Mays and Hank Aaron are retired now, and Roberto Clemente, the great Pittsburgh Pirate, died in a plane crash trying to help earthquake victims in Nicaragua.

None of my friends, Tommy, Burkie or Rosie, collect anymore. I guess I'd be embarrassed if they saw this big box of cards in my room. Tommy'd probably think up some other nickname to make fun of me.

Still, I've finally got a couple things on him. To begin with I really am the only one of my friends that has been kissed by an eighteen year old girl. And what a gorgeous blond girl, too. Ant's a lucky guy to have her. I can't even remember what it felt like, except it was soft and warm and my whole body felt suddenly liquid for a moment, then suddenly electric.

I wish I could describe it more exactly. I do remember the smell of lilacs when she got real close. I can't think of any fresher smell than lilacs. And I remember the softness of her lips as they brushed mine. Not brushed, though, she really did press them into mine. So what if she was kinda making fun of me for staring at her.

The guys thought I was looking at her tits, which are nice and I would like to get a better view of them, but really I was looking at her face. It looked so pretty and soft, my eyes kinda fell forward into it. I couldn't stop looking.

Then she kissed me.

I thought that was everything, but then Linda, who I don't think has ever kissed a boy, and definitely hasn't kissed any of my friends, asked me to walk her home. Out of all of us guys, she picked me. And Tommy even offered first.

I still don't know why she did it, or what it means, but she was nice to me and said she didn't like the other guys, especially Tommy, making fun of me. At first it hurt my pride to have a girl feeling sorry for me, but then she said

I was the only kid that never made fun of her for staying back in first grade. It was like she owed me something for that. I guess I've never had a girl really talk to me like that and be so sweet. It's funny, people always say she's dumb for staying back, but she's smarter than me, I think, smarter than a lot of people. Maybe not in school subjects, but just about knowing things about feelings and important stuff.

Anyway, we promised never to make fun of each other, and that was real. Now I'm wondering if I should call her and tell her me and Tommy are going to be shooting hoops in front of her house later. Maybe I should call and just thank her for saying what she said, or tell her I would walk her home anytime. Maybe she really likes me and I should ask her out, like to the movies this afternoon. I can't imagine what it would be like to sit next to Linda in a movie theatre for two hours wondering if I should hold or even touch her hand.

I could call Tommy and cancel our plans. That would really piss him off if I told him I was taking Linda to the movies, just like that, like it was nothing for me to take a girl to the movies, just like he does. I could call Linda and just ask her.

I don't call. I hover around the telephone with a lump pulsing in my chest. I don't call.


"Pe-ter," the familiar neighborhood call rings out from my porch step. It's Tommy come to get me to play basketball. Ever since I can remember, me and Tommy never knocked on each other's doors, we just stood out front and let out the two syllable call, Pe-ter or Taw-mee, and waited. Our older brothers do it like that, so we did, too.

I open the door and flip my basketball to Tommy and we dribble off down Carter Street, across the big main road and into the neighborhood of our friends, Burke, Rosie and his sister Karen, and Linda.

"Leave it to you to get a girl like Linda alone and just talk," Tommy pronounces.

"What would you have done?" I spit back.

"I would have made out with her," he brags. "I would have at least gotten a good-night kiss."

"Linda doesn't do that."

"Maybe not yet, but she will, and I bet I'm the first."

I hate him. "She doesn't even like you," I stab.

"Oh, so you were talking about me," he grins. "Ten to one, I'll have my tongue in her mouth before the summer's over."

I can't even think about that without a burning flame running straight up my chest.


We shoot baskets and talk about how this year the Red Sox are going to beat out the Yankees and go to the World Series. The hot summer sun trickles sweat off our foreheads and chins. All along we both try and hide our glances at Linda's front door. I see Tommy sneaking looks over there, but I'm sure he doesn't see me doing it or else he'd be making fun of me for it.

Finally, the door opens and Linda gives a sunny wave and smile and sits down on her front step. It's startling to me how pretty she suddenly is. Her sandy hair falls over both shoulders onto her red t-shirt. She is wearing dungaree shorts and no shoes. I wonder if she and Tommy and everyone in town can hear my heart beating.

"Hey Linda," Tommy starts, rolling the basketball to her. "Howard the Coward here tells me you guys made out last night."

"I didn't say that," I protest, like a little kid.

Linda picks up the basketball and stands up, blond hair to bare feet, and begins bouncing it in front of her. Cautiously she keeps her dribble as she moves to the middle of the street, raises the ball up in front of her and lets it go to clang off the front side of the rim and bounce away.

"Huh,ha,ha," Tommy laughs, retrieving Linda's miss. "You shoot like a girl."

For just an instant, Linda's brown eyes peek at me from their corners under smartly arched brows. The beginnings of a smile bloom about her lips.

Then we all shoot some more under the bright June sun.

# THE DEVIL ONLY WANTS GIRLS

I never thought me and the guys would be following the neighborhood girls around, tagging along like puppies after scraps, hungry to learn their secrets, their ways. But here we are down at the end of Clifton Street, where a grove of woods hides us from the adult world, and where the girls have promised to unveil the mysteries of the occult before our very eyes.

Tonight the girls are leading us into the darkness where they say we will witness a trance, an evil ritual in which they will invite the Devil to possess them. Me and the guys are laughing at them, ridiculing them, and following solemnly along behind.

It's not supposed to be like this.

I was getting along just fine being a boy and playing whatever sport was in season, stealing apples, grapes and peaches off the neighbors' trees and vines.

Me, Tommy, Burke and Rosie were kind of a little gang of adventurers. We left our houses right after breakfast and just made up how we spent our days. Back home for lunch and then off again we'd go, creating our own afternoon, with the only rule we had was to be home in time for our parents' suppers.

Even when Karen and Linda started tagging along behind us, nothing really changed much. They really just watched us do the things that we always did. Of course, we noticed that Karen, even at thirteen, was developing in ways that made us guys nervous and excited. Linda was something different altogether. Quiet and pretty, with long rivers of blonde hair, she had a shy innocence we sometimes made fun of in the daylight, but secretly worshipped like something precious and fragile. None of us dared to wonder about her in our darkness beds. She was somehow brighter and truer than that.

Then came that night when Linda asked me to walk her home. I still have trouble believing it all happened, that she asked me, that we spent time together and now have this little sacred bond between us. It's real and it sends soft shivers of electricity through me at unexpected times.

Still, we spent the beginning of our summer as a gang of six. We loped the streets together, us guys in front, the girls a few steps behind. We played basketball, harassed the pimply kid in the ice cream truck, threw rocks at streetlights when we got really bored, and the girls watched us.

Last week everything changed. Dawn broke over our little kingdom and nothing is like it was before. Dawn Daniels, a tall, skinny, black-haired, pale-skinned fifteen year-old, moved into the apartments at the other end of Carter Street and we guys are now the followers.

The funny thing about Dawn is that she is more dusk than sunrise, more night than morning. You can't really call her pretty, but still you look. She's like the flames of a fire that momentarily convince you with their dance, that you could put your hand through them and not get burnt. Then her heat snaps you out of it.

In just a couple of hours, Dawn captured Karen's allegiance with a deck of tarot cards and some black eyeliner. Linda, like all of us, both attracted and repelled, went along quietly. Now there are seven in our group and Dawn is the leader.

Tonight we all flow down the deserted end of Clifton where earlier this summer Tommy, Burke, Rosie and me had our first beers. Now, according to Dawn and her disciples, we are about to witness our first trance.

"The ceremony must be performed in silence," dark-eyed Dawn instructs, peering out from under her black bangs. "Two girls stare into the lighter flame and after a few seconds they start chanting 'Devil come into me, Satan come in to me'"

"I'll cum into her," Tommy asides, snidely.

Dawn stares him down. "Absolute silence is the Devil's song. If you break that silence, I'll know you are scared."

I'm both silent and scared.

"Why just girls?" Rosie asks. "Why can't I do it?"

"Cos you're a boy," Karen answers snottily, a little sister trying to act big.

"With a girl's name," Tommy snipes.

"You gave me that," Rosie gripes, and he's right. It was Tommy who found out his middle name was Roseland, his mother's maiden name. That day Bobby instantly became Rosie. "Seriously Dawn," he continues. "I wanna try it."

Dawn looks at him solemnly from inside those black-rimmed eyes. "The devil only wants girls."

Holy shit.

"Linda," Dawn commands. "Hold the lighter between Karen and me."

Linda looks down at the ground. "I don't feel good," she says. Her face is paler than usual.

"Don't be scared, Linda. Nothing's gonna happen to you as long as you don't chant," Dawn assures.

"I'll hold the lighter," I say. I owe Linda one. We have a secret pact to stick up for each other. Besides, what can happen to me? Like Dawn said, the Devil only wants girls.

"Careful Petey, the Devil wants girls, and you might be close enough," Tommy pokes.

"Oh, just do it, will you," Burke interjects with the authority of being the oldest in our group. "You've been talking about it all day, Dawn."

"Nothing's gonna happen. It's just bullshit. That's why they won't let us guys try it," Rosie asserts.

"Come on, Dawn. Let's show 'em," Karen says, glaring at her brother.

"Okay, Karen, but remember we must invite the Devil in or he won't come. We must want him to come. Now Peter, hold the lighter between us," she orders. Hearing her call me Peter, not Pete or Petey, suddenly tightens a knot in my stomach. This is serious business.

I raise the plastic cigarette lighter up to eye level between Dawn and Karen. Dawn's expression is dark, while Karen's eyes and lips are rimmed with excitement. The other boys and Linda are quiet in the hushed dusk. With my thumb, I ignite the flame.

"Devil come into me. Satan come into me. Devil come into me. Satan come into me." The chant rises slightly in volume each time.

"Devil come into me. Satan come into me." My hand is trembling. The ridges of the metal wheel of the lighter dig into my thumb. The girls remain focused even as the flame dances.

I feel stupidly important to these girls' lives, the keeper of the flame.

"Devil come into me. Satan – Aaaaaaaagh!" Both girls screech and lunge at each other fiercely. Karen whirls Dawn around and onto the ground with a vicious thud. Dawn slaps and claws at Karen from underneath and pushes her up and over onto her back. Karen is still shrieking as she pushes Dawn's face away. Dawn's breathing is a low but loud thrust. She rears up, balls her hands into fists up above her head and, eyes wide, screeches dark and ugly.

Rosie lunges at her and knocks her sideways off his sister and covers her to keep her down. Karen leaps up and on to Rosie's back, still screaming and wailing her fists on his shoulders as Dawn growls and hisses underneath him. Tommy and Burke pull Karen off and away. Rosie yells, "Dawn! Dawn!" into her face from inches away.

"What? What?" she answers groggily. "I'm okay. I'm okay."

Karen is still screaming and trying to tear herself away from the boys.

"Karen! Karen! It's over," Dawn yells from under Rosie.

"What? Wow. What happened?" Karen asks, as she untenses. She shrugs away from Tommy and falls into Burke's arms. "Oh my God. That was intense."

I'm still standing there with the lighter held out in front of me.

Rosie gets up off of Dawn and walks over to his sister who is still collapsed against Burke. "You okay Kar?"

Karen nods into Burkie's chest.

Dawn gets up and brushes herself off, walks over to me seriously and removes the lighter from my hand. She gives me a dark, piercing look that makes me shrink. "Thank you," she says and jams the lighter into the tight right front pocket of her dungaree shorts.

She looks over my shoulder with those same serious eyes and says, "You should try it sometime, Linda."

I turn to see Linda sitting on the ground, arms hugging her knees, face small and lost in a wave of blond hair.

"I have to go home," she says without lifting her head.

"I'll walk you," I say, hopeful. I want to protect Linda, to tell her that everything's okay, that the girls are just faking this whole thing. But, I'm not sure. I'm not sure and I'm afraid and me and Linda are leaving.

"What? Are you guys going out now?" Tommy asks with thick sarcasm.

"Shut up, Tommy," Linda says, lifting her face to reveal water-rimmed eyes.

"Jeez, I didn't mean anything," Tommy says, as we walk away, side by side, in silence. "It was just a joke."

?

"You must think I'm a baby," she says softly when we're safely away from the other kids.

"Oh Linda," I say. "I would never think that." My voice sounds like some bad movie actor talking to a child, or a puppy.

"Don't talk to me like I'm a little girl," she says sternly. "Even though that's the way I acted."

"Oh, I didn't mean it that way, Linda. I just don't like to see you upset." If I were brave, I would hold her in my arms.

"I'm scared. She scares me." Linda's brown eyes, still hidden, face the ground as we walk.

"Oh, it's all fake. She's just trying to be cool and scare everybody."

"But Karen says it's true and she's like my best friend. Why would she lie to me?"

"Maybe she's just trying to impress Dawn."

"Dawn scares me. And maybe Karen's not lying. It looked real, didn't it? They were really hitting each other," she implores, her brown eyes wide open, finally looking at me.

"Yeah."

"So what does it mean?"

"I don't know," I answer, and we walk on in silence. How can I reassure her when I'm not sure myself? How can I be a rock for her when really I'm soft and scared myself? Tommy would have definitely put his arms around her and told her everything would be all right, and she would believe him, because he'd make himself sound believable.

We run across Winthrop, the big, main road and continue into her neighborhood. We walk up Elm to Porter and then turn onto Ford Street, walking side by side in silence.

As we approach her house I stop and pull on her t-shirt sleeve. She looks at me questioningly, her eyes still puffy and rimmed.

"Can I do something," I ask.

"What?"

I lift the bottom of my t-shirt to her face and wipe the tears from her eyes. I feel brave and grown-up and I just want to put my arms around her. I don't.

"Thank you," she says softly.

"Sure."

More silence until we reach her front walk.

"Hey, do you want a grape soda?" she asks.

"Sure. Can we sit on your steps and drink it. You don't have to go in, do ya? It's still early."

"I'll ask my Mom," she says, and turns away and into the house. The long sandy hair falling down her back almost touching her shorts, the butterscotch back of her calves pointing down to red sneakers, the glimpse of Linda in motion, it all entrances me more than the flickering of Dawn's cheap lighter. It eases the unease that has flooded my chest since the trance. They were definitely faking it. Dawn is such a liar, and I know Karen's a big, phony actress. I'm going to tell all this to Linda when she comes out.

She comes out all blond and smiley, freckles.

"We only had one left. We can share," she says, holding out the can. I open it and hand it back to her. She takes a sip and hands it back to me. I put my lips where hers just were and take a drink, sweet and grapey.

"Thanks for not kissing me," she says.

"Huh?" What? I sink.

"Oh, sorry. I don't mean it like it sounds. I just mean when you asked me if you could do something, I thought you were going to try and take advantage of me being scared and like, try and make out and get something off me."

I don't say anything.

"Boys do that, you know. Take advantage when you're sad and start putting pressure on you, and if you did that that would mean that our whole conversation was phony and that you were just like Tommy and Burke and everybody else and just thank you for not doing that."

There is still nothing for me to say. I take a drink from the soda and hand her back the can, looking down.

"That's just not how I want it to happen, ya know?" she says, quieter than before. She's not looking at me now. She's looking down, almost inward. I press my thumb and forefinger together through the bottom part of my t-shirt where it is still damp from when I wiped her eyes. She does want it to happen in some way, some way with me.

"No. I know what you mean," I say, lifting my head, but still looking straight ahead, out to the street and the silent basketball hoop standing guard across the way.

"And thanks for being brave while I was scared," she says, and I feel even better, bigger. I should tell her that I'm scared, too. That Dawn scares the shit out of me.

"Sure, Linda. It's part of our deal, kinda. We stick up for each other, help each other out."

She looks at me solemnly, "Do you believe that they went into a trance?"

"Nah, they're faking."

"Be honest, Petey." Her brown eyes are on me, serious. Her attention is almost too much for me. I have to look down.

"Well, I think they're faking."

"But it looked real and they say it's real," she says, eyes widening again.

"You're real," something in me rises and says. "You're real, and the rest of them are all full of it. Dawn and Karen and Tommy and Burke and Rosie. They're all full of it. I don't know what to believe about the trance, but you, I believe every single word you say."

"They're probably all laughing at me right now."

"No, Linda, they're laughing at both of us. Who cares?" And at this moment, I really don't care what they all think. I don't care what anybody thinks but Linda. "I'd rather be here."

"Me, too," Linda says, handing me the can of soda. "You can finish it."

"Time to come in now, Linda," her mother's voice pipes from inside the house.

"Can't I have five more minutes?" Linda asks back behind her. She really would rather be here, with me.

"Yes, but just five."

Linda smiles at me as if we just pulled off an elaborate scheme, and then turns her gaze upward at the stars.

"Do you believe in Heaven?" she asks.

"Yuh."

Four and a half minutes later we say good-bye, her little smile lighting me on my way back home.

# OUT MY WINDOW

The sun streams through my morning window with a soft choir of birds chirping and chortling in the outside air. The rustle of leaves in the warm summer breeze dances with the rhythm of distant car engines from the big main road. It is the Fourth of July. Independence Day.

I am thinking about Linda.

The other boys, my friends, I'm sure all have their own thoughts dancing in their heads. Burkie's probably waking up knowing, or at least believing that Karen is his girl anytime he wants her, and I'm guessing that he is wanting her right now as he lays in his morning bed, anxious to see her and to get her alone. Any boy would have those thoughts after the way she fell all over him at the trance last night. He could have made out with her right then and there, in front of all of us, and she wouldn't have stopped him. For all I know, that's exactly what happened later on.

Rosie might be thinking about Karen, too, and how he's going to deal with one of his buddies going out with his sister. Going out with – that's a funny term. It's not like they're going to go anyplace. Really it's just a permission slip to make out and do other things. Run the bases, we say. Burkie will have his driver's license in a couple weeks though, so maybe they will go out and have some actual dates. Then it seems like the date is just something to do to justify going parking, which is another funny word, a nice way to say making out and fooling around in a car. Getting it on, as Tommy would say.

Tommy's probably all wisecracks and firecrackers this morning. And girls. He's all about girls, all girls. He's probably thinking about Linda, too, right now, but not in the way that I am. Still, I don't think even Tommy really has any dirty thoughts about Linda.

Linda. I'm thinking about her.

I wish I were just sitting on her front step with a can of grape soda in my hand and her sitting next to me. Her looking up at the stars and my eyes slid to her just enough so that I can see the softness of her cheek, the glistening of her brown eyes in their pools of white, the rivery fall of her sandy-colored hair as she gazes upward into the starry sky. Just that, and some silence as we sit there, and the feeling that neither of us wants the moment to end.

That's not how Tommy thinks of her. To him she's just another pretty mouth to put his tongue in. I hate that. I want to punch him in the face when he talks like that about Linda.

Linda.

I lay back on my bed, with this warm breeze from the windows, these bird songs wafting in, this remembrance of grape soda on my lips, the little damp spot on the bottom of my t-shirt, of her asking me about Heaven, and her eyes rimmed with water, a rising choir of tenderness in my chest, in this room, my room, my little bed, the universe.

I move like a magnet to the window and look out over Winthrop Avenue, the big main road, and into the beginning of another neighborhood, the other neighborhood, where beyond the roof tops and rugged maples, at the fairytale end of a summer street, there is the red brick front step, and the screen door, and inside a whole house, and in that house, one room with one bed, and her in it.

I look out my window a long time.

# BOOM

Tommy lifts the red and white package from his right pocket and then from his left, the matchbook.

"Chickaboom," he says, raising his eyelids.

We are all here, Tommy, Burkie, Rosie and me. And the girls, Dawn, Karen and Linda.

Dawn answers matter-of-factly, "Wow, firecrackers. What a friggin' daredevil."

A little boom pops at her feet as Tommy's first cracker goes off on the hot tar of Clifton Street. Dawn doesn't move except to pretend a yawn. Her hand covers a wide open mouth as her eyelids, smudged dark blue, fall over her eyes.

"Why? What do you got?" Tommy says defensively.

Dawn stretches her pale arms out, displaying her black tank top, dungaree shorts, and long pale legs. "Chikaboom," her dark-rimmed eyes smile.

Everybody takes a deep breath.

"I can't wait for the fireworks," Karen enthuses, leaning and snuggling against a distracted Burkie.

"Why wait?" Tommy asks. He breaks off a firecracker, lights it quickly and tosses it at Dawn's feet. Bang.

She reaches into her little black purse, she is the inventor of the purse in this neighborhood, with these girls, and pulls out a cigarette and lights it. "Pop!" she says with an eye roll, and puts it in her mouth. She is also the inventor of cigarettes in our neighborhood.

"Who the fuck do you think you are?" Tommy explodes.

"Easy, Tommy," Rosie steps in. "Give her a break."

"What? Did she put you in a trance, Rosie?"

"No, but she's not doing anything wrong. She's just not that impressed with your little firecrackers."

Burkie and I look at each other.

"Don't sweat it, Bobby," Dawn shrugs, using Rosie's real name. "I'm not." She turns and blows a plume of dismissive smoke into the air.

"You can have Miss Stuck Up, Bawwwbeee," Tommy draws out the syllables. "I'm just trying to have fun. It's the Fourth of July."

He lights another firecracker and throws it at Linda's feet. She does a little jump into the air and he throws down another one.

"Stop it, Tommy" she calls, jumping back.

"Dance Senorita!" he laughs, tossing another and another at her feet, as fast as he can light them, until she finally breaks into a run. Everyone is laughing but me.

"Why are you such a jerk?" I push out, angry.

"Dance boy!" he yells, tossing one at my feet. That's all I need. I burst into a run and hear Tommy cracking behind me, "Run, Howard! Run, you coward!"

I don't care. I catch up with Linda who is now walking. This could not be better.

"He's so stupid, Peter," she says to me, looking straight ahead.

"Oh he's just trying to show off because Dawn embarrassed him," I chirp gleefully.

"That's the first thing she's ever done that I've liked," she laughs.

"You want to just walk to the park now?" We're all planning to end up there later to watch the fireworks, but it's more than an hour before they get shot off.

"Nope," she says, her eyes looking straight ahead. "I want to run."

Linda takes off, her blond legs leaping forward, sandy hair fleeing behind her. I take off after her, wild and electric. When I pull alongside her we laugh and gasp and laugh some more before finally clomping into a walk.

"I let you catch up," Linda says, grinning.

"I was catching up," I dumbly retort.

"Oh yeah," she smiles and gallops ahead, all legs and gym shorts and blond woosh.

"Okay, okay," I yell. "The Olympics were last year!" I look at her standing there laughing, waiting for me to catch up and I am a firecracker, fuse lit and sparking, exploding at her feet. Bang. She doesn't jump away.


When we get to the park it is already filling up with people. We bump into Ant, Burkie's eighteen year old mechanic friend. I've been avoiding walking past his house for a couple of weeks thinking he might be mad at me because his girlfriend kissed me on the lips. Of course, he's not at all threatened by me, but he might use any reason to give me shit. Something inside me waits expectantly to see what will ruin this miracle evening with Linda.

"Hey Petey," Ant nods to me. "'Bout time you found a girl of your own." With a little chuckle, he and his girl brush by and are off into the crowd. He's not with blond Jenny and her lips and lilac scent. It's another girl clinging to his arm tonight, all dark hair and breasts leaping out of her shirt top.

"Is that the girl you kissed?" Linda asks.

"She kissed me," I protest. "But no, it wasn't that girl. Ant's with a different girl tonight."

"What was wrong with the girl you kissed?"

"Nothing. Why would there have to be something wrong with her? And she kissed me."

"No, I meant why is he not with her tonight. I heard she was pretty."

"She is pretty."

We continue side by side through the park, momentarily silent.

"What did it feel like?" she asks. "The kiss."

"Honest?" I say.

"Yes."

"I can't really remember, it happened so quick," I admit. "But her lips were soft." Linda is asking me about kissing. I'm talking about lips, soft lips. I look at her lips, lips that touched the soda can right exactly where my lips touched.

"I heard she was very pretty," she says, and I wonder who it is that told her about it. I thrill to think that Linda is talking to someone about me. That she cares that some other girl kissed me.

"She was pretty," I shrug. I want to say to Linda, she's not as pretty as you, but that would be stupid, a line from a television show or a movie, but that is what I want to say. I'm looking at her and the comparison is blossoming into truth. That is what I will say if she asks me.

"How can you just go out with someone one day, and like, the next day be just going out with someone else?" she asks. "Like it doesn't even matter who you're with?"

"I don't know." And I don't. I can't imagine right now wanting to be with anyone else on Earth but Linda and we are just talking. Why doesn't Ant feel this way about Jenny? Does he just go out with different girls because he can? She deserves better than stupid Ant. Sometimes I think all girls deserve better than their stupid boyfriends.

"Tommy's like that," she says. "When he couldn't impress Dawn, he came right after me."

"I told him he was a jerk for picking on you."

"He wasn't picking on me," she says. I know what she means and she's right. There's not much for me to say now that isn't childish. I'd prefer the whole night go forward without seeing Tommy or even hearing his name.

We walk along through the crowd, occasionally meeting kids from school or old neighbors, chit chatting idly. It's good. I like to be seen with Linda. It makes me feel big, important.

We get ice cream from a truck parked on the side of the road, its continuous calliope song ringing in the electric summer air.

"Let's see if we can get a good spot on the wall," Linda says and we go. Yes, let's not try and find Tommy and Burke and those guys. Let's not wait for them.

We squeeze in between some people and manage to sit next to each other on the rock wall overlooking the water.

Anyone might think, looking at us, that we're going out, boyfriend and girlfriend. We lap the cold heaven and crunch up the end of our ice cream cones and look up expectantly into the night sky.

"I love how one moment nothing's happening, and then, all of a sudden, it's gonna start. You just don't know when," Linda says, eyes wide and bright.

"Yes," I answer.

In the distance there is a soft boom.

"There it is!" she sparks, pointing across the water. An arrow of white light breaks straight up in front of us and up, up, up until boom, a bright red and yellow flower of lights shower down from the sky.

We watch just silent next to each other, smiling up at the spangling suns exploding across our sky. I tilt back slightly so that Linda's mouth and eyes, bright with joy, light my vision along with the fireworking halo above.

I am not the kind of guy that just goes with one girl one night and then another the next, like it doesn't mean anything. I want to tell her that and other things, all the other things that are inside me that I can't put into words. I want to say to her, that I know her. I know her and I like her and there is a whole world for us that goes out beyond the Whyte Fuel tank and the grove of trees at the end of Clifton Street, that we don't have to settle for the cheap thrills of Tommy's firecrackers or Dawn's trances, that there is something more, something better, something only we understand.

Boom! Brightness, showers of light. Boom.

We keep our eyes up, necks craned, our faces reflecting the glow of the sky. I reach over impulsively, and lightly tug the sleeve of her t-shirt.

"What," she asks softly, never moving her face from the exploding night.

"Nothing," I breathe back.

"Okay," she whispers.

Boom!

# HANDFULL

"Petey, we got a plan," Tommy says, bouncing a basketball in front of him like a point guard surveying his offense. He, Burke and Rosie came to my house right after lunch today. We are making the walk across Winthrop and over to the hoop on Ford Street, across from Linda's. "We'll teach these girls a lesson tonight. By the way, did you get inside Linda's pants yet?"

"Jesus, Tommy. We just watched the fireworks together." It makes me feel big and special to use the word together when it means Linda and me. It feels good that Tommy might really think that Linda likes me, that I'm somebody a girl, any girl, would let in her pants, or near her, at least. And Linda, most of all, who all of us knows is better, somehow, than the other girls, better than us.

"Jesus, Tommy. Just the fireworks," Burkie mimics, arms stretched in mock outrage.

"Yuh, I didn't even notice Linda there beside me," Rosie chimes in.

"Just fireworks, huh Howard?" Tommy chides. The ball still bounces in front of him, his jaw chomps gum along in rhythm. "Chik-a-boom. You should thank me for scaring her off with those firecrackers. I set you right up."

"Yuh, that's all I could think about last night at the fireworks. Gee, I gotta thank Tommy. He's such a great guy."

"I am a great guy. A great man with a great plan. Now listen. Tonight we're gonna get the girls and ask 'em to show us the trance thing again."

"Yuh, we'll ask 'em like we think it's all real" Burke joins. "Then when they go into their fit, we'll just grab their tits!"

"They'll stop for sure when we start milkin' em," Tommy grins.

A free pass to grab Karen's big, firm breasts.

"Burkie'll grab Karen and I'll do Dawn," Tommy smiles.

"Can't we just all do it?" I protest.

"Don't screw up the plan," warns Burke, his face tilting down forward toward me.

"Well, what are me and Rosie s'pose to do?"

"Pete, this is the only way," Rosie explains, taking his turn to lean in and eye me. "Karen's my sister. I don't want everyone grabbing her tits, but she's all over Burke anyway so there's nothing I can do about it. So Burke gets her. Tommy gets Dawn because I already got a little piece of her during the first trance."

"You grabbed her tits?" I marvel.

"Yuh, just one of 'em. By accident. Not like it's gonna be tonight."

"So what did Dawn do when you grabbed her?"

"Nothin'. She acted like she didn't even know it happened."

"Maybe you didn't do it right," Tommy needles.

"Nah, she didn't want to blow her cover," Burke claims.

"So everyone gets some but me," I whine.

"You've got to hold the lighter," Rosie reminds.

"That's not fair," I say. "You could hold the lighter. You already grabbed Dawn. Or I could drop it and then grab one of the girls."

"It's already been decided," Burkie interrupts. "The only way it will be different is if Linda does it. Then you get her."

"She's not gonna do it," I lament. "Besides, if Rosie already got a piece of Dawn and she didn't say anything, how do we know it's gonna work?"

"We don't know. I only got an accidental squeeze. We're gonna find out what these girls do with a full on grab."

"Yeah, when we milk'em on purpose," Tommy chimes.

So, they've already decided without me. Fine. Maybe I don't even go. Maybe Linda and I go off by ourselves, I want to threaten. Who'll hold the lighter then?

"What if they really are in a trance," I say instead.

"Then they won't know we're milkin' em," Tommy says.

"They're not in any trance," Rosie assures. "And this will make them admit it."

"Won't they be mad that we're feeling them up?"

"Karen won't be," Burkie smiles. "And if Dawn is, she'll have to admit she's a liar."

"Yeah, and she is a fuckin' liar," Tommy asserts.

We approach the basketball hoop hanging off the telephone pole across from Linda's house. No one has to tell anyone to change the subject. It just changes.

As dusk whispers into darkness, we all gather and head to the end of Clifton. By the old rock wall, Dawn, her eyes rimmed in thin black liner, assembles and instructs her parishioners.

"Remember guys, you all have to be quiet for the dark spirit to come. Peter, hold the lighter steady. If the flame goes out before the Devil comes, it won't work."

Tonight us boys are more invested in the occult than we were during the first trance, for obvious reasons. Burkie and Tommy are elbowing each other and snickering quietly. Linda is standing a few feet off to the side, head down, quiet.

"Linda, are you sure you don't want to do it?" Dawn asks.

Linda just shakes her head, face still turned to the ground so only her hair answers.

"Tough break, Pete," smirks Tommy. Burkie and Rosie stifle little chuckles.

I could just go over to Linda. See if she'll go for a walk with me. She doesn't want to be here.

"Karen, this isn't the right mood for the dark spirit. We'll have to do it when the boys aren't around," Dawn says.

"No, no, no. We're sorry. We'll be quiet," Rosie assures.

"I'm not gonna do it anyway," I say, partly to make Linda feel better, partly still smarting over not being part of the milking, as Tommy puts it.

"Hold on," Tommy says. "C'mere guys." He pulls us away from the girls, a few yards down the path. "Don't fuck this up," he whispers at me while jabbing a stern finger into my chest.

"What do I care? I ain't getting nothing," I complain.

"Alright, alright," Burke says, "After I grab Karen, if she doesn't stop freaking, I'll let her go and you can grab'em."

I look at Rosie. Karen is his sister. He nods.

"Alright," Tommy says, and pushes me in the chest.

We walk back to where the girls are standing. "I straightened these guys out for you, Dawn," Tommy braggs.

"You'll hold the lighter?" Dawn questions, her dark eyes on me.

"I'll do it, Dawn. Give me the lighter," I say. Linda sits down away from us, wrapping her arms around her knees and nodding her head down.

"Are you going to take it seriously, Peter?"

"Yes," I stammer.

"What were you guys talking about?" Dawn asks, still eyeing me.

"We don't believe it's real," Rosie interrupts.

"Who cares what you believe?" Karen says to her brother, sourly.

Dawn hands me the lighter. "You believe it, Peter."

I'm not sure if those dark, staring eyes are asking me or telling me. I take the lighter from her.

"Remember, steady," she orders me firmly, her eyes lingering on mine. Now she peers around to the other boys, "Everyone must be quiet."

Her and Karen face each other with my hand holding the lighter between them. With a flick of my thumb it starts.

"Devil come in to me. Satan come into me. Devil come into me. Satan come into me. Devil come…aaaagh!" This time it is Dawn that starts the screaming, smashing a fist down on my arm and knocking the lighter from my hand. I jump backward as Dawn grabs Karen by the shoulders. Karen is screaming now, too, and swinging her arms wildly to get Dawn's arms off her. The guys set upon them. Burke from behind reaches around Karen with hands fully clamped on her breasts and pulls her away. Tommy has Dawn in a bear hug, one arm pinned between their bodies grasping at her tits.

"Aaaaaaagh!" The wailing continues. I lunge toward Karen. Burke slides his hands under her arms leaving her breasts exposed in front of me. I clamp my hands on them wildly, and the three of us stumble to the ground.

Behind us Dawn is emitting long gasps from under Tommy, "Uungh! Uungh!" Now a screech and she is slapping at the back of his head and getting free of him. She is loose and leaps on Burkie, Karen and me with a sharp, fierceness in her eyes. Instinctually, I reach my hand out and attach it to her breast as we all roll over on top of her.

Karen rolls off and out of the pile. All three of us guys are now on top of Dawn, pawing at her as she shrieks beneath us.

"Dawn! Dawn! Oh God. Oh God. What's happening?" Karen bellows.

"What? What?" Dawn manages weakly from underneath us. Burkie and me release our grip and we all get to our feet and dust ourselves off.

"That was quite a trance, girls," Tommy laughs.

"Why? What happened?" asks Karen.

Burkie's standing behind her grinning.

I look over to where Linda was sitting. She's gone.

"Where's Linda?" I wonder aloud.

"She can't handle it," Dawn says.

Without a word, I slip onto the path and jump up on the old, rock wall to see if I can see her. I jump down from the wall and begin jogging up Clifton.

"Oh God!" I say out loud as the outcome of this whole evening starts to become clear to me. I'm sprinting as fast as I can now, turning wildly onto Carter, and dashing madly across Winthrop with only a brief glance to check for oncoming traffic. I pass Ant's house on Elm running furiously, gasping, then woosh by Rosie's and curve out on to Porter and then Ford where I see Linda ahead of me, running the last few steps before her house.

I'm too late.

She slows and paces up her walk, onto the front step and into her house. I'm close enough to her to hear the screen door slam.

Oh God. I fucked everything up. Forever.

For a handful of tits.


I am the living statue of an idiot, frozen in the moonlight air. Can't go forward to Linda's, don't want to go back and join the guys who are, undoubtedly, celebrating their moment of triumph. I can't move, a monument to my own stupidity lit for the world by a streetlight. Not even the hungry mosquitos stir me. I let them alone to land, bite and suck. It would be better for me if they could fulfill the slang saying and actually eat me alive. Then at least I wouldn't have to see the look on Linda's face, if she looks at me at all again. The look that says I'm just like Burke and Rosie. And Tommy.

One mosquito too many chomps into me. I smack down on my arm maniacally, stinging my skin and leaving the bug smashed into a smudge of blood on my forearm. This same energy surged through me during the trance as I lunged at breasts.

Slowly I regain my breath, slump my shoulders down and begin the sad, quiet walk back toward my neighborhood.


Tommy and Burkie intercept me on the sidewalk before I cross Winthrop. They are standing under a street lamp laughing and talking.

"Here comes the champ now," Burkie calls.

"Yeah, you milked 'em both," Tommy cracks. "Did you try to grab Linda's, too?"

"Nah, I just wanted to make sure she's okay," I say with non-chalance, as if I had actually caught up with her.

"Why? Because she found out how slutty her friends are?" Tommy pushes out.

"Yeah, we just grabbed their tits full on and they let us just go at it," Burke marvels.

"Even you, Pete," Tommy laughs and whacks me on the bicep. "You got both of 'em."

"Do you still think they're fakin' it?" I ask. Uproarious laughter.

"Of course, they're fakin' it. There's no such thing as trances," Burke lectures.

"So they let us grab their tits cos they didn't want us to think they were faking?"

"No, they let us grab their tits because the little sluts like it," Tommy corrects.

Could they really actually want us to feel them up? Do they like it?

"Yeah, what's Karen gonna let me do when I have my license and we go parking?" Burke exudes.

"Hey, where's Rosie?" I ask.

"He walked the girls home. I think he's pissed at his slutty sister," says Burke.

"You wanna go out with Karen and you think she's a slut?" I ask Burke, myself, the universe.

"Now you're getting it," he grins.

"I'm glad Linda's not like that," I say quietly.

"Don't waste too much time on her, Pete. She's not giving up anything," Burke advises.

"Besides, they're all like that eventually. Once these girls start getting it, Linda's gonna want it, too," Tommy says.

"She's not like that," I mumble. I want to punch Tommy in the face.

"Oh, you're not like that. You'll grab tits if the girls are in some phony trance, but you'll never make a real move on any girl cos your too chicken. I'm telling ya, I'll have my tongue in Linda's mouth by the end of the summer. Maybe I'll let you have my sloppy seconds."

"You don't know her," I protest.

"I know girls," he insists.

I want to either punch the smile off Tommy's face or run home as fast as I can.

"I'm going home," I say.

"Get your squeezers ready for tomorrow night's trance," Tommy jokes. He pantomimes in front of him with his hungry hands.

I turn to cross Winthrop and have to wait for a car full of teenagers to roar by, radio blasting Led Zeppelin, splitting open the hot, blue night. After I cross I walk slowly down Carter wondering what they know, those boys and girls of the summer night. What do they know that I don't? And how did Burkie and Tommy figure this big world out so fast? Did they learn it all after fourteen? Will I be just like them next summer?

And what about Dawn and Karen? Are they really faking those trances? Do they really want us to grab their tits? Well, not me probably, but Burkie and Tommy. And why did I just do it? Maybe the Devil is in us.

That is probably what Linda thinks. She may even think now that I am the Devil himself. But when did she leave? Did she run off as soon as I sparked the lighter? Then she wouldn't have seen me grab at Karen and Dawn.

My house looms up before me. Dawn, and especially Karen, will tell Linda all about anything she didn't see. It's no use.

The night sky hovers over me darkly. It's over. I've lost her.


I go into my house, pass inspection with my parents and pad up to my room with a glass of lemonade. I pull out a shoe box of my oldest baseball cards and bring them up to my bed. On top are the two 1969's that I saved. Harmon Killebrew, the great home run hitter, and Luis Aparicio, the shortstop and basestealer, who I would be, if I could be anyone.

I wonder if the great Luis Aparicio ever acted like an animal with a girl when he was a kid.

I'm so stupid, I think to myself, putting the cards on the table beside me and shutting out the light. Stupid.


"Linda."

I speak her name aloud and crumble to dust under my sheet.

# TELL THE TRUTH

Outside it's the summer of 1977, but here in my upstairs room it is 1966. I'm playing my made up baseball game using index cards which I've filled with information, and which using my own little system, tell what happens when say, the great Roberto Clemente bats against the fierce fireballing pitcher from the St. Louis Cardinals, Bob Gibson. I use real 1966 statistics from my older brother's dog-eared copy of the 1967 edition of Who's Who in Baseball. Every player, every team, every stat.

Outside of my room, the great Clemente is dead, victim of a tragic plane crash, and Gibson is retired. In here, they are in their baseball prime, staring each other down, and the game is on the line. It is the bottom of the ninth, Matty Alou stands on third base, Gene Alley is on second with an improbable double. There is only one out, but the Pirates trail the Cardinals three to two.

I flip the next index card. "Base hit to center field! Alou scores. Here comes Alley around third. The throw to the plate from Flood. He's safe! Alley's safe. The Pirate's win! What a comeback against one of the greatest pitchers in the game. Pirates win four three."

I mark the new statistics in my notebook. Clemente gets two more runs batted in. That gives him 17 and ties him with the big left fielder Willie Stargell for the team lead. The Pirates, which I am managing, are now 26 and 16.

I don't need 1977 and trances and fuel tanks and Tommy's plans to feel up girls and put his tongue in their mouths. I'm staying in.

I flop onto my bed and put my face in the pillow. I can't help thinking about Linda and what she's going to say to me the next time she's sees me. Maybe she won't say anything, just look at me with that hurt and disappointment in her eyes, hurt that I put there by being such a stupid jerk. But probably it will be worse than that. She'll probably act like those nights on her front step never happened, like we didn't sit next to each other on the Fourth of July under the booming spray of fireworks. Like we never really had anything at all.

"Pe-ter!" my mother's voice intrudes from below.

"What?" I bark.

"Bobby's here," she replies, exasperated.

Rosie. What's he doing here? I don't want to have to talk to anyone. At least it's not Tommy or Burke. Those guys would be all about last night and how the girls are all slutty, and how we outsmarted them by copping free feels during the trances. Rosie's not like that. Not all the time.

"Hey, Petey," he says as I enter my kitchen. "Come with me over to Chillwell's and get some ice cream." He's not asking, he's telling me. I glance at my mother.

"I'll get you a couple dollars from my purse."

We go off, but I know Rosie's not here for ice cream.

He starts right away. "Pete, what do think of Dawn?"

"I don't know. She's a little scary and kinda weird."

"What do you mean by weird?" he asks.

"Well, I don't know. She's like, different from the other girls, from your sister and Linda. She seems like she's way older, ya know?"

"Yah, but I like that about her. She's not silly like most girls."

"Linda's not silly," I say, defensively.

"I know. You like Linda. I'm not saying anything bad, it's just…" Rosie pauses like he knows what he wants to say, but doesn't know if he wants to say it. "How was Linda last night after the trance? Did all the tit grabbing freak her out?"

"Nah, she didn't even see it. She just doesn't like the whole trance thing." I like that Rosie just said I like Linda like it's a fact everyone knows, and like it's possible she could like me. I like that he treats me like I'm the person to ask if you want to find something out about her. But I screwed it up, and now I have to pretend to Rosie that everything's all right.

"What?" Rosie sharply questions. "She didn't say anything about it?"

"No, she was cool. We just talked on her front step." I wish.

"She saw, Petey. I saw her see. It was like her whole face got white and she just stared at the whole thing and then she just got up and ran off fast. She was definitely freaking."

"Well, she didn't say anything to me," I continue lying.

"My sister's still pretending that they're really going into trances. I can't believe she just lets you guys do that to her."

"I'm sorry about that, Rosie," I offer dumbly.

"I'm used to it. Ever since her chest grew, everybody's in lust with my little sister," he laments.

"Especially Burkie," I add.

"Well, she loves him," Rosie corrects. "I hope he's not just using her for her tits."

We cross big Winthrop and head up Elm. We'll have to pass Burke's, Ant's and Rosie's then turn on to Porter, go straight past Ford, and on toward the ice cream stand.

"I like Dawn," Rosie says.

"Yah, I guess she's alright. I mean she's kinda scary, but I like the way she doesn't put up with shit from Tommy."

"No, I mean I like her. Like my sister likes Burke. Like you like Linda."

"I don't," I start, but something prevents the lie from rising out of me. "You wanna go out with Dawn?"

"Yeah, I like her."

"So that's why you were sticking up for her to Tommy," I conclude. "Shit. So why'd you let him grab her tits during the trance last night."

"I wanted to see what she did, see if she liked him," Rosie says.

"She hates him, Rosie,"

"All the girls hate him. Then they like him."

Does Linda like Tommy?

"Do you really think Dawn likes Tommy?" I ask.

"I don't know," he says, looking away. "The reason I wanted to talk to you was, do you think she might like me?"

"I don't know, Rosie. I never thought about it." Then I do think about it. "Wait! She calls you Bobby. That's gotta mean something, right?"

"I hope so," he says. "I mean, I noticed that. I like it. It makes me feel like she respects me, or looks at me differently than everybody else. I mean there's gotta be a reason she says Bobby, right?"

"Yeah, I think so. Maybe she does like you," I say.

We continue up Elm. Rosie puts his hand on my shoulder and says, "Alright Pete, tell the truth. I'm telling the truth. You and Linda. What's going on? Are you ever gonna ask her out?"

"Okay," I say.

"Well?" prods Rosie. "Are you going to?"

I say nothing.

"Did you already ask her? Last night after the trance?"

"Oh, Rosie, I fucked everything up. I didn't catch up with her last night," I admit. "I think you're right about why she left last night and it sucks. I think she thought I was different from other boys, and when she saw me grabbing tits last night she realized I'm just another jerk."

"Oh shit," he says. "So you didn't talk to her? You haven't talked to her about it?"

"No, she got to her house before I could catch up to her. Now I'm afraid she won't even want to talk to me."

"You have to talk to her, or you'll have no chance with her at all."

"I'm so fuckin' stupid."

"You? How about me? I decide to like the scariest girl in the neighborhood."

74

"Yuh, Dawn is scary."

"And then I set it up so that Tommy gets to feel her up."

"Me, too," I say through laughs. "Don't forget. I felt her up, too. And she ain't bad."

Rosie raps me on the shoulder. "I'm gonna kill you, Pete."

I take off running down Elm screaming, "Police! Police! There's a mad man after me. He's in a trance!"

"No one can help you now! Satan come into me!" he bellows back in a deep voice. When he catches me, he swings me onto somebody's lawn and we start wrestling around, laughing and brawling.

"Hey you kids," an old woman's voice comes from behind a screen door. "Get off that lawn or I'll call the cops!"

"Call'em ya old bag," I shout and we scramble off down the road laughing and yelling.

# LAST TRANCE

Tommy, Burkie and me gather in the trees at the end of Clifton as darkness descends. Rosie is not with us tonight. He volunteered to babysit his little brother so his sister Karen could come out and our trance experiment could continue.

All day long I've been dreading this. Tommy and Burke are all smirk and adrenaline. Me, I wish last night never happened, that I could just erase it from the history of the world and go back to before, sit next to Linda under a canopy of fireworks and just tell her that I think she's awesome and that she makes me feel special and alive and a thousand things I can't put into words.

But that's dead now and I'm the one that killed it. I want so much to just run home and not have to face her and see the different way she'll be looking at me. The disappointment or the hatred in her eyes, or just emptiness, like maybe she expected me to let her down all along. She always expects to be let down by boys, by the world I think, and I proved her right.

In the distance, the girls appear. Dawn in the middle, Karen and Linda on either side. They really are breathtaking, walking toward us in the summer heat. Gone is the bragging and name-calling we boys do when we huddle alone. None of us speak a word.

"Hey Peter," Linda bubbles, as the girls approach. "I bet you can't wait for tonight's trance."

"I bet you can," I say, trying to be confiding, but sounding more like Tommy than the boy I want to be when I'm with Linda.

"No, I'm doing it tonight," she smiles, almost mean, almost sad. This is terrible.

I pull her away from the others and say paternally, "Linda, you don't have to do this. Don't let Dawn pressure you."

"Nobody's pressuring me, Pete. I want to," she says and pulls away from me. "Everyone makes their own decisions."


Tonight I'm the one that gathers the guys together away from the girls in one last effort to save things with Linda, to save my life, or at least do the right thing. "Look guys, if Linda does it, no one grab her tits, okay."

"I'm milkin' her," Tommy starts. "And if you don't like it, go home with Rosie. You got 'em both last night."

"No, Tommy, let Pete do it," Burke says, using his authority as the oldest. Turning to me, he warns, "But you have to do it. We have to prove they all like getting felt up and that they're lying about this trance shit."

I nod my head.

"Alright, but if you don't grab 'em, I will," Tommy warns.

I want to be done with this, to go back to a few days ago, before this ever started, before Dawn moved into the neighborhood. I want to just sit with Linda on her front step under a big moon and share a grape soda.

I nod my head and we return to the girls.


"Okay. Okay," Dawn calls us to order. "Tonight Linda is going to call the Devil in with Karen. I will hold the lighter."

Linda stands determined at Dawn's left while Karen, at her right, tries poorly to conceal a bubbling excitement. This is really going to happen.

Dawn flicks on the flame of the lighter and the chant starts.

"Devil come into me. Satan come into me. Devil come into me. Satan come into me."

Tommy looks straight at me, his lips upturned at the corners. Burke poises to pounce on Karen.

Through my head flashes the solution. I will grab hold of Linda immediately, pull her to the ground and cover her until it is over. She is better than all this. If Tommy wants to give me any shit when it's over, I can claim to have gotten a piece of Linda in the scuffle. But Linda will know the truth. And Tommy won't have his hands on her.

This thought lifts me. I'm saved. Linda's saved. There is a rising in my chest that releases from my lips in slow, cool, long breaths.

"Devil come into me. Satan come into me." I watch Linda's brown eyes, sweetly serious and set on the flame. I make a promise to those eyes, to myself, our old promise, and I'll keep it.

"Aaaaagh," The girls begin screeching. Linda leaps at Karen and I nearly catch her midair, roll with her to the ground, free my left hand as I lay on top of her and firmly grab and squeeze her right breast urgently.

"Oh God, what happened?" Linda quickly yells, breathless. Oh, God. I let go and quickly scramble to my feet. Promise, heart, everything – broken.

Dawn stands over Karen who is screaming and wrestling with Burke. "Karen! Karen! It's me Dawn."

"Whah?" Karen foggily answers, and its over.

I offer a hand down to help Linda up, but she rises on her own and turns away from me, dusting off. What does she need me for now?

Dawn looks over at her and she back at Dawn.

Tommy throws his arm around me and chides, "Looks like you're starting to like these trances, Petey. Hey, Linda," He juts his chin toward her, "Wanna go again?"

"No," Linda says, chin up. "One's enough for me."

"I don't blame you," I say.

No response.

I blame me. The same kid that sits beside her bursting with thoughts and feelings and that I can't even say, the same kid that doesn't even have the courage to hold her hand, and I can't even stop myself from getting a free feel off her. I'm just another boy to her now, a boy that takes advantage of her. There is no return now to her brick front step, to the grapey taste of soda on my lips, to her.

"I'm going for my license next Saturday," Burkie announces.

The conversation changes. The dense air lifts. We act like friends.

# HEELS AND WHEELS

"Pe-ter!" The familiar two-syllable call rings out from my driveway. Tommy is standing outside my kitchen window pounding a basketball into my driveway. I haven't seen him since the night of the last trance. All week long I've been in my room, or going for walks down the end of Clifton Street, not the side with the stone wall and the wooded path that leads out to the fuel tank, but the other side, where the ruins of an old factory stand beside a wide, reedy field that winds its way down to the river.

It's a spot I've always liked to get to by myself, to kind of talk to myself out loud with nobody hearing me. It gets me away from my room when I'm down and I'd like to just cover up and cry. It let's me avoid the guys hassling me to hang out when I just want to be alone. It puts me out of ear shot of my parents' voices grating on me about why I haven't been outside lately, or why I'm not out with the other kids playing hoops or whatever sport is in season.

This week it's been a place for loud self-punishment and quiet feelings of shame, for being very sorry for myself, and longing, sadly, to see Linda. It is where I go when I'm missing her and our little sacred promise most.

"Hey," I say to Tommy. "I don't feel like hoops today." Not the hoop that is hanging across from Linda's house, from that brick front step, that girl whose lips used to share grape soda with me.

"C'mon, you haven't done anything all week," he says. "Besides maybe Linda will come out and watch us."

"Nah, let's do something else." Something away from Linda.

Tommy puts the ball under his arm. "Hey, you want to see that new James Bond flick?"

"Sounds good," I say. "Gimme the ball. You can grab it on the way back."

I stash the basketball in a closet in my house and ask my Mom for movie money. "Well, I'm glad you're finally leaving the house," she says. "But that room's got to be picked up this weekend."

That room, I think as I head out the door. Which room are you talking about? I want to ask to be a wise ass, but the ten dollar bill between my fingers smartens me up. I haven't been in the house anyway. I've been in that room, my room.

I let the screen door slam behind me and we head off up Carter toward Winthrop and the movies.

"Maybe we shoot a little after," Tommy says, then smirks and brightens up. "Hey, I never asked you. Whose got the nicest ones? Karen, Dawn or Linda?"

"Don't be a jerk, Tommy." I seriously do not want to talk about the whole trance thing, me and Linda.

"I'm serious. You grabbed 'em all. Who's got the nicest set?"

"Who knows? It was all over their clothes and everything. Besides, my heart wasn't in it," I say half-heartedly.

"Bullshit!" Tommy calls me. "You were into it as much as anybody. Maybe more. You even went after Linda's. I don't think I could have done that. I mean she's…"

"She's better than our stupid little games," I fill in.

"No, I just didn't think she'd really do it. I thought she was innocent, thought she'd just slap anyone who tried to touch her. Turns out she wants it just as much as any of these other girls."

"Shut up, Tommy."

"Shut up, what? You grabbed her tits." His hand slaps against my chest, pushes me back.

"I shouldn't have. I didn't want to."

"You wanted to. You're just sorry cos she's not the angel we all thought she was. I'm psyched. It means she fair game."

"You don't even know her," I lash at him. "Stop talking about her like she's a whore."

"Listen Prince Charming, you're just like me," Tommy starts, tapping my chest with his finger. "You want it just as much as I do, but the truth is you're too afraid to do anything about it unless you get a free shot like the trance. At least I'm honest about. I'll have my tongue down Linda's throat before school starts, you'll see."

He's completely right about me. I hope he's wrong about everything else.

"I don't care," I lie. It's all I have left that doesn't make me sound like a baby. "Karen's got nicer tits anyhow."

"Yeah, Burkie's a lucky guy. Going for his license today, too. Then he's got it made. He'll be screwing her before long in the backseat of his parents' station wagon." He pauses to chew on that thought and then asks, "Hey, what do you think of Dawn's."

"Pretty nice," I say. There's no use. I just go along.

"Yeah," Tom answers. "And she's easy."

This is why I've been hanging inside all week. I don't want to talk about girls or hear about girls. All I want to do is sit next to Linda like before and look up at the stars. I've lost everything.

We hook onto to Winthrop and cut along the sidewalk to the big Sack Cinema movie theatre. Four shows in one building. It's a Thursday afternoon, so it's a little quiet, mostly teenagers and some Moms. We step up to the window and buy our tickets to For_Your Eyes Only, the new James Bond flick. We step inside and head for the popcorn counter.

"Holy shit," Tommy grabs my shoulder and whispers at my ear.

"What?" I say, annoyed. If I was bigger I think I'd beat the crap out of him for always shoving at me and punching my shoulder or my chest. We've fought a couple of times as kids and he's always won. One time he had me on the ground and could have really started beating the shit out of me, but he just said, "Okay, Petey?" like a question. I knew what he meant. He got up off of me and the fight was over.

"Dawn," he breathes. He juts his chin toward a spot just over my shoulder. I glance around to see what he sees.

"Jeez," I gasp. She is moving down the sidewalk toward the ticket window, high-heeled in a short black skirt and tight white shirt. It's something my mother would call a blouse, white and tight, showing off the shape of her tits.

Her hair falls over her left shoulder, a dark river. From her right shoulder, a little black purse hangs neatly.

"Yeah," he laughs, whacking my shoulder, never taking his eyes off Dawn. "C'mon."

He pushes by me, away from the counter and back out the door, me tagging behind.

"Hey Dawn. What's up?" He asks in a voice that is not as cool and non-chalant as Tommy usually uses.

"Me," she says. And she is up, with her heels, like 4 inches above me and a couple taller than Tom. Her smile is from some glamorous ad in a ladies magazine, like the ones my mother picks up at the supermarket check out.

"What are you doing here?" Tommy asks. I'm just silent, awed.

"You didn't think I go to the movies?" she smiles.

Tommy's insulted. "What are you? Too cool for 'em?" He takes everything she says as a challenge.

"I'm here, aren't I?" she says. She shakes her head, an adult marveling at the silliness of children. Looking down toward me, she continues, "Hi Petey, what are you guys seeing?"

"For Your Eyes Only," we answer in an awkward unison. We are children talking to a woman.

"I'm going to see Exorcist Two," she states, eyes widening, chin up and proud, over us.

"You have to be seventeen," I chirp. Little kid.

She extends her arms out shoulder level allowing us to behold all of her. She makes a very good point.

"You'll never get in," Tommy sniffs.

"You guys want tickets, too?" she asks.

"Nah, we've already got ours. You go to the movies by yourself?" Tommy asks.

"No, I'm meeting my friend Gina, from Taft." Taft is where she lived before moving to our town of Endicott this summer.

"Well, I hope you and Gina like James Bond," Tommy smiles.

Dawn lets her purse slide off her shoulder and into her hands. Looking down at us she says, "This is your last chance to exit PG world and see an adult movie."

"You ain't gettin' in," Tommy tells her.

"You still doubt me?" She smiles and glides past us, looking more like someone who might be in a movie than a ticket buyer. We can't hear the conversation at the ticket window, but her face is cool and confident. After a few words she reaches calmly into her purse and produces some bills and slides them through the slot to the pimply kid who has probably just fallen in love with her. Back through the slot come the tickets. Dawn places them in her purse, smiles pleasantly at the pimply kid, turns to us with a satisfied smile, spins on her heels and glides away from us to the door that opens to the other side of the theatre lobby where the R rated movies are shown.

Tommy and I stand silently on the walk for a moment. "Let's go into the movie," I say opening the door to re-enter our PG world.

"She thinks she's hot shit," Tommy snears. She is. She's hot shit and we both know it and I, for one, would have no idea what to do with it.

Tommy and I both enjoy the Bond flick. He laughs and pounds my shoulder every time anyone mentions the woman star's name, Dr. Goodhead. The villain's name is Jaws, like the shark, and his mouthful of silver fangs is funny and menacing, but half the time I'm thinking about what's going on in the other theatre, wondering what Dawn is seeing in Exorcist II that the world thinks is too adult for Tommy and me. It can't be just that it's scary. There has to be something else. But while I sit here in the darkness watching Bond slip into and, miraculously, out of trouble, I can't think of anything more troubling, more intimidating, than Dawn, herself.

After the movie we spend a couple minutes standing around on the front walk of the movie theatre hoping to see Dawn and her friend Gina, but they are nowhere to be found. We give up and start our walk down Winthrop back to our neighborhood.

"I didn't know Dawn was so hot," Tommy says. "She looked like a college girl, or a model."

"Yeah, I didn't know what to say to her," I admit.

"Oh you don't know what to say to any girls," he points out correctly. "Besides, she's just a girl and you've already grabbed her tits."

We walk on silently. When we get back to my house, I go inside to get Tommy's basketball, passing by my mother like she's furniture.

"Well, how was the movie?" she asks, a little offended.

"Good," I monotone on my way back out the door. It's a neighborhood code we have, me and all my friends, to tell the parents as little as possible.

I hand Tommy his ball and he tosses it back to me with a little behind the back flip.

"Let's play some hoop before supper, maybe Linda will come out, she's more your speed."

My speed? I'm stuck in neutral and I don't know which direction to turn. Thump, thump, thump, I dribble the basketball in front of me. "Okay." What else am I going to do? I've got to face Linda sometime.

"Just cos she looks twenty…" Tommy says absently as we walk along. "I mean if she wants to prove she's a woman she can definitely prove it with me." He whacks at my shoulder again.

I wonder if I should tell him that Rosie likes Dawn. I wonder if it would even matter. And, would Rosie want me to say anything?

"She makes Karen and Linda look like little girls," He continues, more to himself than to me.

"I think Rosie likes her," I say.

"Well, he better hurry up, because I'm going to find out just how adult she is."

"Why don't you give Rosie a chance?"

"You know he likes her?" Tommy asks.

"Not for sure, but I think so." I can't tell him. Rosie will kill me.

"Well, he better hurry up or I'll beat him to it."

"You think you're gonna get every girl."

"It's good to have goals," he grins. "By the way, you better get to it with Linda, too."

"You want Linda? You can have her," I say stupidly.

"Oh, what happened Romeo?" he asks.

Don't you know, Stupid. I'm an animal who grabbed her tits like she was some tramp. I grabbed everybody's tits. I can't control myself. I'm like you, Tommy. And now I'm sure she hates me.

"Nothing," I say. "I'm just saying if you want to put your tongue in her mouth, just do it. Who cares?"

"Great. Just don't be all mad at me when it happens."


Finally, we reach the basketball hoop and start shooting. I love just running in and flipping up reverse lay-ups, scooping the ball backward toward Tommy, bouncing out for a jump shot. Basketball's a great sport because you can have almost as much fun goofing around as you do playing a game.

A screen door slams behind us. I turn to see Linda standing on her front step, her hair in two long braids, one on each side. She gives a sunny wave and I immediately wave back, "Hi!" I can't stop myself. Seeing her for just one quick moment pushes all the horror and doubt and sadness away. All the hopelessness, the trances, Dawn, Tommy – all gone.

"You look like you're about ten with those pig tails," Tommy yells to her.

"We must be in the same grade," Linda replies.

"No, suh. I didn't stay back," Tommy answers.

I just stand there looking at her for another moment. "She's smarter than you, Tommy," I say.

"Oh, Peter, you're so in love. Why don't you ask her out?" Tommy prods.

I take a shot, like I didn't hear him, and it clangs off the rim. Linda walks over to us, dungaree shorts and bare feet. Tommy flips her the ball and she shoots. It bounces of the backboard and into the hoop. Two points.

Linda lifts her arms straight up into the air, fists clenched in celebration, heels raised off the ground, balanced just on her bare toes.

Boom.

"Lucky shot," Tommy chides. He flips the rebound, up and in, and then tosses the ball back to Linda. She clangs the next one and we all get our turns to shoot and show off.

Beep, Beep. A horn blasts repeatedly. It's a woody station wagon rolling up Ford Street toward us. Behind the wheel and the blaring horn is Burkie, America's newest driver, wide grin on his sunny, blond, face.

Tommy, Linda and I clap and whoop it up as he pulls along side us. "You got it!" Tommy shouts.

"Just call me Wheels," Burkie answers. "Get in. Get in."

We all pile inside. Tommy grabs for the front passenger seat right away. "Big kids in the front. Little kids in the back," he chuckles.

Fine with me. For the next hour, Burkie tours us around the familiar streets of Endicott in his parents old station wagon, transformed into his new big toy, our big rolling box of laughter, joy, and music.

The little kids in the back and the big kids in the front harmonize as one, through huge smiles, to the "hoo…hoo" chorus of the Rolling Stones "Sympathy for the Devil".

# WHO ARE THOSE GIRLS?

It's Sunday afternoon and I'm drying lunch dishes in my parents' kitchen, thinking about yesterday, me and Linda shout-singing in the backseat of Burkie's station wagon. Everything is going to be alright. In fact, I have this sunny feeling that it's all going to be great.

Waah! Waah! I hear a horn beep, beeping out front.

I move to the window and see Burkie in his parents' woody with Tommy along in the passenger seat. This is a first for me. Someone out front in a car to pick me up that is not a parent or a relative. I'm going out with my friends in a car.

"Oh, it's Burke," my mother gushes from her spot at the kitchen table. My father gets up from his rocking chair and the two of them go outside to congratulate Burkie on his driver's license.

"I'll be right out," I yell through the screen to the guys. I head into the bathroom and comb my hair, looking at my scrawny self in t-shirt and dungaree shorts. I run my fingers across my hair. I better look as good as I can. We're a carload of boys now. Anything can happen.

"Have fun kids," my mother tells the guys.

"But be careful," my father adds sternly. The two of them walk back up the driveway. We pass each other with goodbyes.

And away we go.

Burkie spins us around town in the early afternoon heat and light, the radio playing, the laughs just rolling out. We're not doing anything differently than we usually do when we walk around the streets of our neighborhood, giving each other shit, bragging about girls, whacking each other on the shoulder.

The car is our new toy, a toy we don't know how to use just yet, but we know it's potential. As we toodle around town, it's not just what we're doing that excites us, it's what we're going to do.

"We should go to Vincent Beach next weekend," Tommy enthuses. Vincent Beach is a big ocean side amusement park. We've all been there many times as kids, but always with parents. This will be our first chance to hang out there, just the guys.

"Yeah," Burkie answers. "Let's bring the girls."

"Have you ever been to Vincent Beach?" Tommy asks, pulling his head back in surprise. "There are girls there. That's why we're going. Why bring a sandwich to a banquet?"

"Cos I like the sandwich that I'm bringing," Burkie grins. "I want to eat it."

"Aren't you taking Karen out tomorrow night?" Tommy asks.

"Yeah, to the movies."

"And parking," I add.

"You got that right," Burkie grins. He's shining from the driver's seat, chin up like old pictures of Franklin

Roosevelt from our social studies textbook. All he's missing is the long cigarette holder between his teeth.

"Speaking of movies, you should have seen Dawn yesterday," Tommy says.

"She go see James Bond with you guys?"

"No, she went with some girl from Taft."

"Really. Was she nice-looking."

"We never saw her. She was meeting her inside," I say.

"But we sure saw Dawn," Tommy notes

"Yeah, she went to see the Exorcist Two."

"How did she get in?"

"High heels and make up," Tommy answers.

"She looked like she was twenty," I put in.

"Seriously?" Burke asks.

"Wo!" Tommy shouts, as Burkie wends the car back toward our neighborhood.

"What?" Burkie adds.

"Did you see those girls on the railroad bridge?" Tommy asks.

"No, wait." Burkie swings the car into an empty driveway and backs out the other way so we can head back in the opposite direction.

"Look. Look," Tommy points.

"Decent," Burke declares.

"Oh, yuh," I nearly whisper. There are three girls standing on the railroad bridge that crosses the river where we swim sometimes.

"Who are they?" Burkie wonders as he pulls the car over. We jump out and move to take a closer look. There's one blonde and two dark haired girls.

"Nice!" Tommy says. We cross a parking lot leading to the railroad tracks.

"Who are those girls?" Burke asks again. One of the brunettes pulls her t-shirt over her head to reveal a bikini top.

"Wo ho!" Tommy chirps.

The girl puts her hand to her nose and jumps off into the water.

The blonde pulls her shirt off as well. She stands on the edge of the bridge considering her jump. That's Linda.

"Wait a minute!" I say.

"Those are our girls," Tommy realizes.

Linda lifts up on her toes and splashes into the water.

"Still don't want to bring'em to Vincent Beach?" Burke chides Tommy with an elbow to his side. Dawn leaps off the bridge and joins Linda and Karen in the water. We watch as all three of them climb out and back up onto the bridge. The sight of the three of them standing there in their bathing suits stops us cold. The three of us marvel at the sight, our feet planted in the dirt at the edge of the railroad tracks.

"I never knew they looked like that," Tommy gasps, sounding like I usually do, like an amazed kid. We all just stand there looking, admiring.

"Do you think they look at us the way we look at them?" I ask.

"Me, maybe. Not you," Tommy laughs and punches my arm.

"Let's go ask'em to Vincent Beach," Burkie decides. Me and Tommy don't object.

We amble down the railroad tracks toward the girls, trying to look cool, like characters in a movie.

Karen looks up and notices us coming and shoots her arm up in the air, hand fluttering frantically like an anxious teacher's pet in class. "Hey Burkie!"

"Hey," the other guys respond, still trying to act nonchalant. So they're pretty and wet and in bikinis. What's the big deal? Me, I'm silent and a little stunned, not in one of Dawn's phony trances, but in a real one.

I just look at Linda. The other girls are very pretty. Who could say which was the most beautiful? I look at Linda, trying not to stare. I don't even say hello. I don't know what to do.

"Do you like my bathing suit," Karen curlicues to Burke.

"How was the Exorcist?" Tommy asks Dawn.

I'm still silent, looking at Linda. She smiles sunnily at me. I don't know what it all means or what I should even say. I take two steps to the side and leap into the water, shirt, shorts and sneakers still on. Underneath the water, I can barely wait the second or two it takes to splash back up through the surface. I raise my arms up like a champion. "Woohoo!" I whoop.

Linda leaps off after me, then Dawn. Everybody's laughing. Burkie and Tommy peal off their t-shirts and pull off their sneakers and follow. Karen splashes in after, falling almost into Burkie's arms.

"Well, are you even gonna say hello?" Linda asks me, drops of water glistening across her freckly smile.

I just smile and shake my head back and forth. She whooshes a splash of water at my face and the night and the summer nearly explode.

This is it! This is what I always imagined the older kids were doing on Summer Sunday afternoons. This is how I want my life to be.


Now, we all agree to go to Vincent Beach next Saturday. Talk turns to rollercoasters, ferris wheels and fried dough. Tommy's no longer worried about bringing sandwiches to banquets. He's doing cannonballs and dives off the bridge, trying to impress Dawn, I'm sure, while she acts unimpressed.

I feel sorry that Rosie is missing out on all of this. Sunday is the day he spends with his Dad.

"Hey, why didn't you go to your Dad's with Rosie," I ask Karen, who is huddled close to Burke.

"Why don't you mind your own business, Petey," she snides back.

Linda is walking the railroad rail, arms outstretched to balance herself. I'll mind that business.

"You could be a gymnast, Linda," Dawn marvels.

Of course, I think. Or anything else. Everything else.

Linda tightropes toward me. "Ouch, this rail is hot," she says stepping off next to where I'm sitting. "Feel," she says, looking down at me and placing her foot flat against the skin of my arm.

"It's melting," I say, cradling her foot with my two hands, causing her to lose balance. She steadies herself by placing a hand on my shoulder.

"See," she says.

"Yeah," I nod. I could hold the warm skin of her foot in my hands for the rest of the afternoon, until the sun sets and rises again. Through the next rain, the coming of Autumn and the leaves dropping off the trees. Through the frost, the freezing of the river. The first snowstorm. We will walk home across the frozen ice to get warm socks and boots for her feet.

Linda lifts up her foot from out of my hand and stands at the edge of the bridge.

Splash! That's her. The next splash is me.


Later, after the late afternoon sun dries us all off, Burkie offers to give the girls a ride home in his parents' station wagon.

"Nah, we're going to walk," Dawn says, and Linda and Karen agree. They gather their things and head one way, Linda up on the rail again, Dawn trying to follow along behind her, but with less luck. Karen keeps turning around to look back at Burke.

Me and the guys head down the tracks the other way, back to Burkie's car. We're just silent for several steps, not having to say anything, like cool guys in a movie

"Summer's awesome," Tommy says, almost to himself, like a priest giving blessing.

Yes, it is.

# DRINKING AND THE DEVIL DON'T MIX

I head past my parents in the kitchen. Rosie is at the door. It's Friday night, time for this week's version of our new summertime ritual. All summer long, Burke, Rosie and me have gathered down the end of Clifton on Friday nights to wait for Tommy and his brother George to roll up in his big, blue car with beer. I missed last week, when I thought all was lost with Linda.

Tonight there is no Burkie. It's his first weekend night with a driver's license and he is going to spend it taking Rosie's sister Karen to the movies. The Sack Cinema is really just a short walk up Winthrop Avenue, but Burkie is surely making a big deal of pulling up in front of the O'Leary's house, opening the passenger side door for Karen, wending out of the neighborhood, and then cruising up Winthrop like a rock star. He looks the part with his shaggy, blond hair, and with Karen clinging to him like an adoring young starlet, he probably feels the part.

With his parents' car and his driver's license he is leaving our walking around world and passing through a garage door into a new world that is bigger with possibility and also smaller because of what is now within his reach, the steering wheel. After the movie, when he's parked out at the beach with Karen, he will be on a different planet. Tonight he drives a spaceship.

"I can't believe it," Rosie mutters, after we reach the stone wall. "My little sister's out on a car date before me. I'm sure she's going parking with him afterward, too. Burkie said they have a reservation down at the beach. Asshole." There's a place everyone calls the beach, back behind a bowling alley, even though no one ever swims there. That's where kids around here go parking, after the obligatory movie. "She'll probably let Burke do whatever he wants to her. I tried to get my mother to make her come home early, but she acted as if everything was fine."

"Yuh, has she seen what her daughter looks like now?"

"You're not helping," Rosie grumbles. He picks up a rock and casually uncorks a long throw, across the street and deep into the reeds that lead down to the river. "Then I'm gonna have to hear about it from both of them."

"Burke's a good guy," is all I can think to say.

"We're all good guys," Rosie says. "Good guys who throw girls down in the dirt and grab their tits."

"Yeah," I agree. "I feel like shit about that. It's like I really had a nice thing with Linda and I screwed it up by acting like an animal. I mean, I was with her Sunday, you know, and everything seemed cool, but it wasn't the same, I don't think. We had a blast driving around in the back of Burkie's station wagon, singing to the radio the day he got his license. Then Sunday I saw her swimming down at the railroad bridge. It seems like she still likes me, but now she knows this bad thing about me. I don't know. I can't believe she doesn't hate me for it."

"She's not dumb, you know. She always knew you were a boy," Rosie says with a tired smile.

"Yah, but she didn't think of me like Tommy or Burkie. She thought I was different."

"You are different."

"I think so, too, but I didn't act any different during those trances. She must think I'm a jerk."

"We are jerks," Rosie agrees. "None of us were any better than you. I almost want to apologize to Dawn for it."

"Apologize to Dawn?" I ask, not getting it. "She started the whole thing."

"Not the tit grabbing. That was us," Rosie reminds me.

"Yeah, but she deserved it, trying to bullshit us with that trance shit. She had Linda scared shit at first," I say.

"She didn't deserve it. She was just trying to fit in with us, get noticed. She's new in town. She was trying to impress us. What would you do if you moved to a new town and had to try to make new friends and fit in?" Rosie reasons.

"You really like her, don't you?" I pronounce. I've been trying to find a way to tell him about seeing Dawn at the movies yesterday, and about Tommy.

"Yeah," he answers, looking off distantly toward the road where we expect George's big boat Impala to come rolling up at any minute. "Yeah." He picks up another rock and hurls it high and long. It buries itself deep in the reeds with a whispery whoosh. "What the fuck is taking Tommy and George so long?"

"Me and Tommy went to see the new James Bond yesterday, and she was there."

"She?"

"Dawn."

"Did she see it with you?" he asks, suddenly all alive.

"No, she went to the Exorcist Two." Just the facts.

"The Exorcist. Holy shit. How'd she get in?" Rosie marvels, now even more smitten.

"She just bought her own ticket. She was all dressed up in high heels and a skirt. She looked like a model. You should have seen her."

"Like a model, huh?" Rosie says, almost to himself. "Hey, who was she with?"

"She was meeting one her friends from Taft."

"Girl?"

"Yeah, yeah. Gina was her name."

"What did Tommy say?"

"Nothing. We never even saw the girl. She was meeting her there."

"No," Rosie shakes his head. "What did he say about Dawn?"

"At first he said she wouldn't get in, but then afterward, he couldn't stop talking about her."

"Like, what did he say?"

"Just that she was hot and that she looked like a college girl," I reply. I've already said too much.

"You didn't tell him that I like her, did you?" He sets his eyes right on me.

"No," I lie. "But I wanted to tell you that I think he likes her."

"Of course he likes her," Rosie barks. "He likes 'em all. Does Dawn like him? That's what I need to find out? Does she like him?"

"I doubt it. He such a jerk to her."

Rosie waves his arm at me. "That's all an act, and she knows it. He's just like that because she stands up to him. She's not like most girls."

For sure. "I think you better ask her out before he does," I advise.

"I was gonna ask her to the movies tonight. Maybe double date with my sister and Burkie."

"Why didn't ya?" I ask.

"I don't know. Why don't you ask Linda to the movies?" He turns things back on me.

"That's different," I say, though it is not different at all.

"Yah, right," Rosie says. "You're just scared of being rejected."

"So are you," I blubber.

"I know. That's what I'm saying. At least I'm admitting it," Rosie affirms. Neither one of us wants to give up possibility, the thing that keeps us awake and alive in the darkness at night. Once a girl says no, that chance, that dream, is gone. It goes, leaving us alone in our empty midnight rooms, knowing no hope will rise with the morning sun.

"My sister told me you jumped in the water with your shirt and sneakers on," Rosie says, grinning.

"Yeah," I smile sheepishly. "When we got there I just couldn't stop looking at Linda. It's not that she's prettier than the other girls she's just... I don't know."

"You like her."

"She makes me, like, fall apart sometimes, you know? And she was just smiling right at me. I didn't know what to do, you know?"

"So you jumped off the bridge," Rosie laughs.

"Yeah," I laugh, too. "Right off the bridge. Sneakers and all."

"Jesus, you're more scared than I am. Good thing there was water there. I'm glad you weren't standing on a roof or something, you fuckin' nut."

Rolling towards us now, down Clifton, is George's blue Chevy Impala, Tommy grinning in the front passenger seat and holding up the beer.

"It don't take much to scare the shit out of us," I say to Rosie.

"Nope. Just two pretty girls."


It's not long before the beer starts working. I've heard my dad say something about death and taxes being the only certain things in life. Really it is death, taxes and beer.

"I sure wish I was Burkie tonight," Tommy laughs, whacking Rosie on the arm. "Whaddya think he's gonna do with your sister in that station wagon?"

"Who cares? What do you want me to do about it?" Rosie growls. He gives Tommy a solid punch to the shoulder.

"Jeez, nothing. I was just fooling around," Tommy says, making a big show of rubbing the spot where Rosie's fist landed. "I did hear that that back seat goes all the way flat, though."

"Good. Maybe Burke will let me borrow it for your hearse," Rosie answers.

"Hey, have you guy's seen Ant's new girlfriend?" I ask, aroused by all this parking talk.

"Yeah," Rosie says, "Huge knockers."

"Me and Linda saw her the night of the fourth. Linda thought she was the girl that kissed me." I love to say me and Linda. It makes me feel like I have something the other guys don't, and like I'm old enough to really talk with the other guys about girls.

"Yuh, I saw her. Her tits were jumping right out of the top of her shirt. I'd like to get her in a trance," Tommy laughs.

"If she jumped up and down they'd probably come bouncing right out," I say.

"Sproing!" Tommy shouts.

"Yeah, you could just reach right in," says Rosie. "Scoop'em out like ice cream."

"I still think he's crazy for dumping his old girlfriend," I admit.

"She had you in a trance," Rosie chuckles.

"Satan let me come into her," Tommy shouts.

"What about Colleen in a trance, Rosie?" He has always been in lust with Ant's older sister.

"Oh yeah. Wow."

"Stare into the flame, Colleen baby!" I rave.

"How 'bout Farrah Fawcett?" Tommy asks.

"No! Wonder Woman," I laugh.

"I'd love to see Linda Carter do that change from regular chick to Wonder Woman, and when the smoke clears and everything, she's got no clothes on," Tommy barks.

"Yeah!"

"Wait guys. This is it," Rosie says. "Jaqueline Bisset in a trance."

"Jaqueline Big Set," Tommy roars.

"Yuh, her and Linda Carter in a trance. Petey you hold the lighter," Rosie yells.

"Oh my god, Jaqueline Bisset in The Deep," I gasp.

"Holy shit. That wet t-shirt."

"That was a great movie."

"What jugs!"

"You could just play it with the sound off."

"In slow motion."

"Oh, god!"


I open up my fourth beer. The other guys are already half way done with theirs. This is our little trick on George. Usually he gets us a twelve pack, and when Burkie is here, that means three beers apiece. Tonight there's only three of us.

In the distance we see two girls walking down Clifton toward us. Rosie stretches out his arm in front of him, finger pointed at the end. "Here comes Dawn and Linda."

"Wo!" Tommy says. The beer makes his voice louder than I think he wants.

They move closer to us, talking and laughing with each other. Suddenly, in the moonlight, both all leggy in dungaree shorts, hair falling on their shoulder, smiles and sandals, they don't look so different from each other. Just two pretty girls.

I say those words in my head knowing the phrase is really a lie. They are pretty, they're girls, and there are two of them. It's the 'just' part that's a lie.

To Rosie, it's DAWN. Dawn coming near. And that is everything. To me it's LINDA. Linda is around and my feet leave the ground. She is everything.

"How's the beer, boys?" Dawn asks.

We answer with a mixed chorus of goods, greats and heys.

Dawn steps in front of Rosie and smiles. "Can I have a sip, Bobby?"

"Sure," he says, stretching out his arm to hand the bottle to her.

She takes it, puts it to her lips and tips it back slowly. After a long tug, she wipes her lips with her other wrist and hands it back. "Getting kinda warm," she says.

"You drink?" Tommy questions.

Dawn shoots him a glance, "Still doubting, huh?"

"So you didn't like the Exorcist yesterday?" he asks her.

"It sucked. It wasn't even scary."

"For Your Eyes Only was great," Tommy boasts, as if he made the film himself. "Especially Doctor Goodhead."

"Ha. Ha," Dawn fake laughs. She has a way of moving her eyes up and to the side that makes me feel like she knows a lot of stuff that we don't.

"You're just mad cos you wasted your money on The Exorcist," Tommy continues.

I'm half listening, half trying to think of something to break the ice with Linda. It seems the more I like her the harder it is to talk to her.

Tommy holds out his beer in front of him. "Hey Linda? You want to try it?" He's given up on Dawn, I think. Now he's trying to aim his tongue for Linda's throat, just as he's promised.

"I guess I'll taste it," she says. She lifts the bottle eye level and looks at it. After a deep breath she puts it to her lips and takes a small sip.

"Uuhh! That's gross," She blurts, her head and shoulders erupting into a quick shudder. We all laugh.

Tommy takes the bottle back and finishes it. Rosie offers the last inch of beer in his bottle to Dawn.

"No, you drink it. I'll help Petey with his."

"I don't need any help," I sniff back, insulted.

Dawn does a little curtsy in my direction. "May I have a sip, kind sir? You would be helping me."

I hand her the bottle. We pass it back and forth until it is empty. Sometimes Dawn's just like a regular kid.

Rosie kicks at the box of empty beer bottles at our feet. "Now what?"

"I've got an idea," Tommy says, with a thrust of his right fist. "To the top of the tank!" He wants to climb the Whyte Fuel tank, like he, Burkie and Rosie did earlier this summer.

"Alright! I've never been up there," Dawn says.

"You're going to the top of the tank?" Tommy questions. With a backhand wave he gestures toward me.

"Aren't you gonna stay down on the ground with Howard the Coward?"

"What do I have to do to get you to stop doubting me?" Dawn asks, smiling right at Tommy.

"We'll think of something," Tommy snides. "What about you, Linda?"

"No way," she shakes her head. Awesome, I think. Me and her together. The rest of them can climb the Stairway To Heaven for all I care.

"C'mon, Linda. It will be good practice for the rollercoaster at Vincent Beach." We've all made plans to pile into Burkie's station wagon and head to the Vincent Beach Amusement Park tomorrow. Burkie's license is opening up all of our worlds.

"That's different," Linda says. "On a rollercoaster you're at least strapped in."

"Going a hundred miles an hour," Rosie says.

"Linda, you promised me you'd do it," Dawn says.

"Yeah, I will, but I'm not climbing the tank," she finishes.

"Maybe if Howard here goes, she'll go," Tommy says, draping an arm over my shoulder.

"I'm fine down here," I answer.

"Me, too, Tommy," chimes Linda. "Why does everyone have to do what you want?"

"I'm just invitin' ya. Jeez." He takes his arm off me with a little push. "Stay on the ground. Me, Dawn and Rosie'll tell you how awesome it was later."

We make our way through the grove of woods. A hot line of flame drips down my chest as we pass the little area where we gathered earlier in the summer for the trances, where the girls pretended to be possessed, and where I at least was. I can't even look at Linda, remembering what I did.

"Time for a quick trance tonight, girls?" Tommy prods.

"Drinking and the Devil don't mix," Dawn says. She always has an answer, one that is impossible to question.


Linda and I crane our necks back, looking up as the others climb up, up to the top of the tank. A quick wave of dizziness knocks at me, making me take two quick steadying steps.

"Are you drunk, Petey" Linda asks, lending a steadying hand to my shoulder and looking me in the eyes with the concentration of a doctor.

"Nah, it's just the looking up that got me off balance."

"Let's sit down," she says. We go over to a rock by the edge of the woods. Tommy, Dawn and Rosie are on top of the tank.

"I could never climb up there," Linda says.

"Hey look!" Tommy shouts from the top of the tank. "It's Howard and Howardette. K-I-S-S-I-N-G!"

We are not kissing.

"Let's go," Linda says, standing up.

"What?" I look up at her startled.

"Let's just go. You know he's gonna be a jerk to us when they come down."

Okay. This is awesome. Have your beautiful tank top view, I think. Then something else comes to mind.

"Hey, you know what's funny. Dawn's wearing a tank top on a tank top," I chuckle.

"Oh, what? Are you in love with her, too?"

No, I'm in love with you, I want to say. "Not me, them," is what I say instead.

We make our way back through the woodsy path, past the trance spot, and out to the old rock wall. I stumble and almost fall trying to climb over it. Clumsily, I straighten up on the street. Linda puts her arm around my shoulders to steady me.

"You need some ice cream," she diagnoses.

"Mrs. Robinson, you're trying to seduce me," I giggle. I can only make jokes about me and her ever being more than friends. Anything more true and serious is too scary.

"Do you have any money on you," Linda asks.

"No, and I can't get it at my house. My parents are home and I don't want them to smell beer on me."

"We'll go to my house," she says. "I'll get some from my mom." Good. I'll follow you anywhere.

We walk along up Clifton talking mostly about the amusement park at Vincent Beach. There are all kinds of rides and games there, fried dough and cotton candy. All the kids in Endicott, heck, in Massachusetts, think of it as a little heaven. It will be the first time we've gone there all together and without our own or somebody else's parents along to grate on us and keep us from having too much fun.

"Did you really promise Dawn you would go on the rollercoaster?" I ask Linda as we meet the sidewalk of Winthrop, the big, main road. We run across seriously even though there are no cars coming.

"Yes," she says "But you don't have to."

"I'm not gonna. I don't care about getting made fun of. But why are you doing it?"

"I guess I just want to prove to Dawn that I'm not a little baby," she says.

"Now you're in love with her," I joke.

"She tried to get me to go to the Exorcist Two with her, but I was too scared," she says.

"Scared of the movie, or of trying to get in? Or of Dawn?"

"All three," she smiles.


We get to Linda's house and we see her mother puttering about in the glowing yellow of the kitchen window, where she always seems to be.

"Hey, Mom. Can me and Petey have some money to go get ice cream?" Linda asks from the front walk.

"Oh! You scared me," comes the response. "I didn't even know you were out there."

"Well, can we?" Linda asks again.

"Is Chillwell's even open this late?" her Mom wonders.

"It's not even ten yet and it's the weekend," Linda points out.

"Oh, alright, Linda. But you two come right back."

Linda goes inside to get the money. As I stand on the walk I wonder what her mother thinks of me, what she thinks we are, what we do together. I wonder if the two of them talk about me. She doesn't seem at all surprised when the two of us show up alone. Except, of course, when Linda's voice rises from the empty darkness to startle her, like just now.

When we get to Chillwell's Ant is there leaning against the fender of his Mustang, arm around his girl, licking a vanilla cone. His girl, her tits eyeing us from the top of her super tight blue shirt, is slurping chocolate chip.

"Good night for a lick, huh Petey," Ant grins.

"Yeah, yeah," I say, hurrying by.

"How come you two aren't double dating with Burkie, now that he's got his license?" he continues.

"Already seen it," I say over my shoulder, meaning the Bond flick. Oh yeah, and me and Linda aren't dating. I'm afraid to ask her out.

Linda looks up at the big board that lists all the flavors. "What are you gonna get?" she asks.

"Maple crunch," I say. "Medium."

She keeps looking up at the menu. I like the way her skin furrows up right above her eyebrows as she reads through the flavors. "I want chocolate chip, but I want maple crunch, too."

"Get chocolate chip," I say. "We can share. I like chocolate chip, too."

"You're a genius," she smiles.

Just standing next to Linda waiting for the ice cream that we are going to share with each other is a thrill. I could do this every night. Or just this one night lasting forever.

"Karen's going way too fast with Burke," she says.

"Yeah," I answer. What else can I say? I don't want to go fast at all. I just want this and maybe holding hands.

Can I kiss you goodnight? That would be enough for me. I like you, Linda. I don't say anything.

"And Ant's girlfriend's shirt is way too small for her," she says.

"No comment," I say. I regret that as soon as it leaves my mouth. If I weren't still a little drunk I wouldn't be trying to be funny. I'm so afraid Linda will bring up the trances and just lash out at me about grabbing everybody's tits, about grabbing her tits. I can't even believe I was on top of her on the ground, in the dirt, with my fists squeezing her tits through her shirt like a wild animal. Some part of me thinks her being nice to me is all an act leading up to an explosion against me where she just tells me we could have had something nice, something special, but I fucked it all up by being such a jerk and an animal. She has every right to hate me.

The ice cream comes. We walk along back toward her house slurping seriously and finally crunching up the last ends of our cones. "Hey Petey," Linda starts, her eyes looking up at me as her tongue rescues some maple crunch from the side of my cone. "Why'd you jump in the water with all your clothes on last week?"

"I don't know," I shrug. I can't give the real reason, that she knocked me out with her sweetness. Her sunny smile knocked me right off the bridge. "Let's go swimming now," I say instead.

"I don't think so, Mark Spitz," she answers, referring to the gold medal Olympic swimmer. "You heard my Mom."

"Hey what do they call Mark Spitz when he drinks too much?" I ask, grinning sillily.

"Um…let me think," she says, rolling her eyes up to the sky.

"C'mon, it's not that hard."

"Wait, wait..." She shakes her palm at me. "Mark Pukes!"

"Yes! You're the genius now!"

"Did you just make that up?" she wonders, eyes bright and wide.

"We made it up together. You had the same punch line I was thinking of."

"Hey, yeah," she realizes. "You don't have to puke do you?"

"No, no. The ice cream did the trick, just like you said it would, Doctor."

"Just doing my job."

"We're a good comedy team," I say, but that's as far as I dare go. Tommy would probably have his tongue down her throat now. Why did I let myself think of Tommy, of him kissing Linda, when I'm right here with her? This was Linda's idea to go off alone together. She must like me. Right?

As soon as we get to the walk in front of her house Linda's Mom calls to her, "You should come in now, honey. Goodnight Peter."

Linda cups her hands around her mouth and puts her lips so close to my ear that I can feel her breath. "Be super quiet, and just go around to the side of the house. The window on the corner is mine," she whispers. "See you tomorrow, Pete," she says loudly as she backs away, for the benefit of her mother's ears. She raises her eyebrows and slides her eyes left, an arrow for me to follow.

"Bye Linda," I say, my line in the script.

I sneak around the side of her house, my heart tumbling and summersaulting across my chest. I wait, wait, wait an interminable few seconds. Is she really going to come or is this a trick? Then her door opens. She switches on the light and closes her door behind her.

"Hey," I whisper.

She hears me and shuts off the light behind her. She comes over to the window and puts her face down close to the screen. "Hey," she answers, smiling. For a few seconds we are just there lighting up each other's darkness. Just a thin screen separates our faces.

"If you don't want me to go on the rollercoaster tomorrow, I won't," she offers seriously.

"No, it's alright," I say, melting.

"Okay, but I'll stick up for you if Tommy starts being a jerk about it."

"Thanks, but I'm used to it," I say. Used to that, but not used to this. Her breath touches the skin of my cheek.

Moments go by silently, sweetly. The room behind her lightens as my eyes adjust.

"This is like confession," I say. She and I and our whole neighborhood are Catholic. We've all been raised on the ritual of confessing our deepest sins in a dark booth to a priest who listens behind a shadowy screen.

Linda furrows her forehead the way I like and begins speaking in her deepest voice, "Tell me, son. What are your sins?"

"Bless me Father," I squeak. "But tonight I got drunk and peeped into a girl's bedroom window." Little giggles squeeze from our mouths.

"Say one million Hail Mary's," Linda intones deeply. More giggles. We work to compose ourselves and be quiet.

"Nice Andy Gibb poster," I smirk.

"I love him," she confesses. I guess now I'm the priest.

I croon out the title line from his new single, I Just Want To Be Your Everything, in my tinny, silly falsetto.

"Ssshhhh!" She whispers through giggles. "You gotta go, or we'll get caught and I won't be able to go to Vincent Beach tomorrow."

"Okay, okay," I say.

"Goodbye. See you tomorrow," she tells me quietly, brightly.

"Goodbye. Goodnight," I whisper finally. Goodnight feels brave and right. She gives a little bent hand wave as she pulls the shade down between us.

I sneak and slip out of her yard, rising so far above the Earth that no matter how far down I look, I can't even make out the top of the Whyte Fuel tank below.

# WATCH OVER HER, ANDY GIBB

That was a beautiful, long, moony walk home.

It was as if I stepped from Linda's yard and rose like a bird into the dark night sky, soaring up, then gliding across the neighborhood houses and trees.

Or even calmer. I stepped aboard a slow boat, drifting effortlessly on an easy, wending river. The streets, the trees and houses, moving backward underneath me, around me. The whole Earth whispered about me, promise.

Back home in my room, I open up a notebook to a blank page. Someday I'm going to write a letter to Linda that will tell her everything I'm feeling about her, all she means to me, but I can't do it yet. Now, at the top of a piece of notebook paper I can only write the beautiful beginning – Dear Linda. I look at those words a long time, and then I tear the sheet from the notebook and put it in the top drawer of my clothes bureau.

I see those words as I close my eyes, I see her. I'm lying in my bed now under a cool sheet with my window open and the lightest of breezes wafting in through the screen. Me, my room, in fact the whole house, is at rest in an easy whisper. Everything is a whisper, a secret fluttering through a window screen.

Linda is in her room now, a room not so far away, a room I now know. Lucky Andy Gibb watches over her from above. What a fortunate place for him to be. If I could never move again, I can't think of a better place to find myself stranded than on the wall above her bed spending the long nights watching over her as her guardian.

Do a good job Andy, in your sacred duty.

She is either asleep now or awake, thinking about me or not. It's all right either way. It is all right. She is a maker of promises, a keeper of secrets. She takes care of me. She nursed me through my little three and a half beer buzz, protected me from Tommy's jokes.

That is, at the very least, like. It has to be.

I could lie here awake all night, not sleeping, not tired, just thinking about her. I want to. She may be the only girl I know, the only girl I've ever met or seen. The only real girl. Everyone one else seems imaginary, fictional, as real to me as Jaqueline Bisset or any of the other gorgeous actresses we were joking about and drooling over earlier. I could just as easily imagine making out with Farrah Fawcett as I could with Dawn. Not the impossibility of it, just the distance. Dawn is as different and as far away from my world, my thoughts, as any movie star. She's like a different species from a different planet.

Sometimes I think all the other kids are in a different world. Maybe not Rosie, but definitely Burke and Tommy and Dawn and Karen. That's okay with me tonight. I like this world. I like Linda's world, our world, the moon and the stars.

I wonder what she's thinking of now in her room not so far away. She saved that rollercoaster thing for me, that offer, that little promise. She won't ride if I don't want her to. She won't leave me alone if I don't want to be alone. But it's okay, I told her. It's okay. I won't be alone. I have her promise. I have all our little promises and secrets. I am not alone. Even if she's way up there on a rollercoaster and I'm way down below, I carry her with me.

This is peaceful, perfect. I only wish she was here with me. I imagine lying next her, what it feels like to be next to her, her lying next to me. Not here, not in bed. No, I imagine us together in a field, lying out under the midnight sky, maybe in the reedy, long grass field by the river, looking up together at the stars. At peace. Giggling. Getting each other's jokes. Each other.

And she is in her bed now, right at this exact second. My whole world, my thoughts and secrets, the inside of my innermost self, my heart, my girl, the one girl, the only girl, the real girl. Everything. Here in this bed, or there in hers. Nothing else matters.


Watch over her Andy Gibb from your fortunate post. Do your job well, until the day comes that your job is finally mine.

# NOWHERE TO GO

Saturday blooms like always this summer, bright and blue skied. That's the outside the window report. Inside my room, blue skies, too, fair weather. Downstairs I go early, to have Rice Krispies and orange juice. I am up. Snap, crackle, pop.

Tommy comes by this morning to call with the familiar "Pe-ter", and we head out for our adventure, sprinting across the big, main road to make our way over to Burkie's.

"Are you getting it on with Linda or what?" Tommy asks, as always, interested in only one thing.

"Nah, it's not like that," I say. I can't possibly explain what it is like to Tommy. What me and Linda are like. He wouldn't understand.

"Where'd you two go last night?" he asks.

"She wanted to get ice cream," I say, innocent, mysterious. I can't help but enjoy this, Tommy interested in my social life.

"And then what?" he pries.

"Then we just did what we always do," I say, my voice a mixture of pride and non-chalance.

"Oh, so nothing," Tommy snides. "You still think she's too good to fool around with? You'll never stop being afraid of girls."

I hope that's not right. Never is a long time.

We get over to Burkie's and the rest of the gang is already there. Karen slides into the front passenger seat next to Burke. Me, Tommy and Rosie spraddle into the back seat, me stuck on the hump in the middle. Linda and Dawn sprawl behind us in the way back of the station wagon. Burkie rolls it out of his parents' driveway and off onto the road toward Vincent Beach, our first big car adventure without parents.

The ride is full of laughter, wisecracks and radio. We sing along to songs by Ted Nugent, Peter Frampton and Queen. When the disc jockey mixes in Under My Thumb by the Rolling Stones we all belt it out, Linda and Dawn all hair and holler behind us.

Tommy leans up to chide the front seat couple. "Hey, how was the beach last night? I mean the movie."

Burke responds by spinning the volume nob on the radio, filling the car with Mick Jagger's boasts, and the churning engine of the rest of the Stones.


Burkie pulls the woody wagon into a spot in the Vincent Beach parking lot and it's here we go. The warm, sugary smell of fried dough and the oily aroma of Italian sausages broiling with onions and peppers envelop us as we buy our tickets and crash into our sunny amusement land.

The tilt-a-whirl is the first ride we see and we all scramble on, spinning helplessly around, circles inside circles. I don't like this sort of thing, being controlled by some carnival machine, or at best some toothy teenager with a lever in his hands, earning extra money on the weekends, probably just mulling over come-ons for each pretty girl in his line, not paying attention to us dangling around at the mercy of his fingertips. I'd rather be standing solid on the ground, but I can only take so much coward shit from my friends.

Linda sits next to me on the dark ride as corny, fake monsters flash out, our car careening along a curvy track. Burke and Karen start making out as soon as they sit in the seat behind us.

We wander along through the midway. Tommy stops to try and knock some bottles over with a baseball, but has no luck.

"It's rigged," He pronounces. Of course it is.

Rosie pulls me aside as the others stand in line for a ride called The Round-Up. "I'm gonna do it on the roller coaster," he says. Everyone has agreed that that is going to be the last ride of the day.

"Do what?" I ask.

"Ask Dawn, or something," he says. He's awkward and unsure of himself, but at least he's got a plan. I'm not even sure Dawn likes him, even though she always calls him Bobby. Last night it seemed like she was flirting a little with Tommy, all this 'you still doubt me' stuff.

"Right on the roller coaster?"

"Yeah," Rosie says. "On the way up. I'll just lean over and ask her out."

"Sounds good," I say.

"So when are you gonna ask out Linda?"

"I don't know. I kinda like what we've got now." That's true.

"You're just scared," he shoots back. That's also true.

The rest of the gang is up on The Round-Up whirling around. I watch Linda as the speed of the ride whips her sandy hair behind her. When the big wheel comes to a stop they all stagger off in various states of dizziness. Burkie slips his neck under and between Karen's legs and straightens up so that he carries her up on his shoulders. She bounces above him, proud and giggly, down the midway.

Ahead we see a bandstand where guys in white suits are playing horns and belting out old time swing music like from movies my mother used to watch in the afternoons while folding clothes or doing the ironing. Those movies almost always had some big nightclub scene with a band playing. The singer was always in some kind of trouble, either owing money or being chased by two different guys.

Anyway, the band is blowing away this old swing music and people are up in front of them dancing. Karen and Linda ask us all to wait for them here while they go off to the bathrooms. We give the band a polite hand when the song stops and then they launch into another.

Dawn sways around a little to the music. "Anyone want to dance?"

We all stand stiff like stones. Tommy chuckles and says, "My Grandmother dances to this."

I not so subtly elbow Rosie. This is his chance, I think. Make your move. He pushes me back hard instead, almost knocking me into Dawn. She grabs my hand and pulls me. "C'mon Petey. It's only a dance."

We edge into the crowd, wriggling around. She's can really dance, of course. It seems she's good at everything adults do. We laugh at each other's surprising moves and steps. It's fun. When the music stops Tommy and Rosie roar and egg us on for another song. We sway and step around each other like lunatics, laughing and clapping our hands as the white suits play on. When we finish Dawn opens her mouth and eyes in a wide, wild smile. She places her hands, one on each of my cheeks, lifts up on her toes, and plants a kiss on the middle of my forehead, laughing.

"You guys are alright!" Rosie exclaims. It's the first time I haven't felt intimidated or even actually scared of Dawn since she moved to the neighborhood. I can kinda see what Rosie sees in her.

The girls get back from the bathrooms and we go in to see The Human Crab. Linda and Karen eek and back away as the poor guy opens and closes his deformed claw feet and scuttles along from side to side. Dawn rolls her eyes and yawns. It's no show really, unless you count freak show, and it leaves us all feeling ripped off and sad at the same time.

"What a jip," Tommy moans, disgusted at paying money to just see the poor guy.

"It's not the guy's fault," Rosie protests.

"I know," Tommy admits. "I feel sorry for him, too, but they should have a sign up that says nothing's gonna happen."

We move on and catch up with Burke and Karen. He's trying to toss little rings onto bottle tops and win her a stuffed animal. Another rip-off. We head to a little food corral and order up some fast food cooked on trucks in oily vats. It smells good, tastes okay, and probably shortens our lives by a month or two.

Next is the dodgems. These are all rides that seemed big and cool to us when we were younger. Now Burkie is actually driving an automobile and next summer Tommy and Rosie will have their licenses, too. Linda and I spend our time trying to control our cars long enough to get a little speed up and smash into each other without getting knocked off course by the other drivers. Burkie and Karen are, of course, in the same car. He's just spinning it round in circles trying to get her dizzy.

Walking down the midway, as the afternoon moves, Linda half whispers to me, "You sure it's okay if I go on the rollercoaster."

"It's your funeral," I joke.

"Don't say that. I'm scared enough as it is," she smiles back. Wisps of her sandy hair fall across her eyes giving off a kind of shyness.

"Well, just don't worry about me. I'll be hanging out with the human crab," I assure her.

"Oh my God! Did you see his feet?"

"Or whatever they were."

"I know!"

"How does that happen?"

"His parents must be some lookers."

Finally, it's rollercoaster time. As they all wait in line, I slide away to find a fried dough stand. They could almost charge you just for the smell of the butter and the bread cooking. I get the big, warm piece of dough, beautiful, with a soft dusting of powdered sugar, and launch into it as I walk back toward the rollercoaster. I'll choose this sweet, doughy chunk of heaven over holding on for dear life and getting the shit scared out of me, every time.

As the monster coaster comes into view, I can see the gang heading up the long slow rise, Burkie and Karen in the front car, Rosie in his heaven with Dawn in car two, Tommy, probably aggravating and frightening Linda in the back.

I grab a seat on a thickly painted bench and watch them rise up the long slow climb of track that every coaster has to heighten the fear and excitement before it sends you dashing downward, screaming and careening. Just before they reach the top, Burkie pulls Karen into a kiss. Behind them Rosie throws his arm around Dawn and makes his move, mouth to mouth.

And in the next car back, Tommy throws his arm around Linda's shoulders and starts kissing her. As the car crests and falls over the top of the coaster, my world goes with it. I see them, Linda and Tommy, kissing. Then they disappear.

Everything disappears. An inferno rises up from my stomach, straight up through my chest and engulfs my head. The water rimming my eyes cannot cool the heat or blur the image in my mind. I bolt up and whip my half-eaten fried dough at the ground. I see a blond girl passing by with a boy scrunch her face and say, "What's wrong with him?"

Everything. I want to just run, run full speed, somewhere, anywhere.

There's nowhere to go.

# DEAD PLANET

I stand here alone in this eternity, a dead planet with a fun house mirrored universe spinning around me. Words blare at me, wind up jack-in-the-box music screams, faces appear and distort, yell and squawk. The windows of my heart have shattered and fallen to the pit of my stomach, a pile of broken glass. I am empty, alone, a stranger to all of this.

"Any ring on any bottle gets your choice," a huckster calls out from his stand. "What about you, sir?" he eyes me through the crowd.

My choice? How the fuck is anything my choice.

"I'm so drunk," a girl's voice giggles behind me. Everybody now has what is gone from me and they flash it in front of my face.

"Haha! Let's get in line!"

"Step up! Step up! A winner every game!"

Not in this one.

Things don't stop when you do. Everybody else's worlds whirl by in their merry orbits, mine teeters and halts, ends. So this is why Linda wasn't afraid to go on the rollercoaster. She wanted to go on.

A thousand years later, one second later, after everything ends, and is pronounced dead, the rollercoaster rushes to a stop. The cars empty. Burkie, Karen, Dawn, Rosie,

Tommy and Linda all burst from the ride noisily laughing and screaming.

"Oh my God," Linda opens wide in front of me. "I am never doing that again. It's soooo scary!"

Liar, I want to scream back in her face, fuckin' lying, phony bitch. I say nothing.

Somehow I get my feet and legs moving under me and slide into the flow of the group. They banter and laugh about the rollercoaster, not noticing my crumbling, my rage, the quaking of my heart inside me.

"Aaaw, someone dropped their fried dough," Linda says sadly, finger pointed to the ground with the same hand that just last night waved goodnight to me through her window screen.

That's you and me on the ground, Linda. That's where you left us, threw us down. Or just me. That's where you threw me down.

The car ride home is forever, a nightmare dripping slowly like blood from a cut. Wipe it away and here comes another red stream creeping across my skin. No one speaks to me or about me. I'm a mannequin propped up in the back seat as the others all live.

"Andy Gibb!" Linda bursts from the way back as his new hit single scratches from the radio. She nudges my shoulder from behind. So, big deal, you know I'm alive. 'I saw you fuckin' kiss him, liar!' is what I want to scream. I don't turn around. I don't speak. I don't even move.

When we get back to Burke's I give a cursory wave, mumble "See you later," to no one in particular, but to everyone really I'm saying goodbye. Don't see me later. Any of you. I want to run full speed.

Tommy rushes up behind me for the walk back to our neighborhood, laughing and pounding me on the shoulder.

"I told you! I told you!" he bellows. He punctuates everything with a punch or a shove.

I struggle along, walking rapidly, pretending not to feel Tommy's pushes and punches.

"Didn't you see me?" he questions.

"What," I bark. If we are ever going to fight again, me and Tommy, it is going to be now. He might have let me off easy the last time, but if I could just get one good one in now I wouldn't care if he beat the shit out of me.

"Didn't you see me?" he says, eyebrows raised high over his beaming, stupid smile.

I pick up the pace of my walk, not replying, looking up ahead of us, away from him.

"Don't tell me you didn't see it! I made out with Linda!" he exclaims.

"So…" I spit. Is he trying to kill me, or is he so caught up in his own stupid Tommy world that he doesn't see how angry and sad I am?

"So, I told you I'd have my tongue down her throat before the summer's over," he brags.

I could punch the conceited grin off his face. "So what!" I blurt. "Are you going out with her now?"

"Of course not. I don't even like her," Tommy says. "I'm gonna go out with Dawn."

"So you're gonna screw Rosie over, too," I seethe, nearly spitting in his face as I snap off the t in too.

"What are you talking about? Screw over?"

"You know what I mean." You won't get me to say it. You have to say it, to admit what you did, what you're doing. The heat around my ears is an inferno.

"If you wanted to kiss her you should have just done it," he shoots at me. "You had plenty of chances."

He's right. I did have chances, dozens of chances, and every time I chickened out. I waited, I cowered. Howard the Coward. I always knew that Tommy would know what to do with Linda, not me. I blew it.

"Did she like it," I ask, punishing myself.

"Of course she did. All girls like it, no matter what they say. The trances should have taught you that. Now I'm going to see if Dawn will put her money where her mouth is," he smirks.

We run across the big, main road. I want to cry.

"You should be happy. I don't even want to go out with Linda. I just broke her in a little, like a baseball glove," he pleads innocent. "Now she's ready for you," he pushes at me and pounds his right fist into his left palm, like a shortstop does before crouching into position. "And let me tell you, she's a good kisser. For a beginner."

"Who cares? And what about Rosie?" I say, just completely pissed with Tommy, Linda, life.

"That's not my fault, either. He kissed Dawn on the roller coaster and she didn't like it. It's not my fault that she likes me better."

I slow to a stop and stand still in my tracks wanting to push Tommy, to take a swing at him. I want to beat his fuckin' head in. I just stare down at the ground around my feet.

I can't be here anymore.

130

"Fuck you!" I yell and take off running toward my house, toward my room, toward my bedroom, my bed, and under the covers where I will stay, where I do stay the rest of the afternoon, through supper, through Saturday night.

"He must have had too much fried dough," my mother tells my father in their house beneath me, in their world. I am not in that world or any other. No one has told them that I am broken, gone. They mistook the ghost that stumbled past them and up the stairs for the me that they used to know.

The real me is nowhere, and that girl that I thought was real, the one from across the big main road, over the roof tops, behind the window screen, in the sacred secret darkness – she no longer exists.

But that is not true. That girl does exist and she is in the very same place as she was last night, but that's all that is the same. This night she does not whisper promises through window screens. This night she lies in bed, probably dreaming of Tommy, flush with the taste of his tongue in her mouth, his lips on her lips. Everything that came before today, everything else, was a lie.

The first thing I did when I got into my room was grab that letter I was going to write from my top bureau drawer, that letter that started Dear Linda. I was about to write another letter, full of anger and hurt and disappointment, but what would she care? I just left the piece of paper on my desk, unchanged.

I could tear that page in two, but she doesn't even deserve the effort. She's not thinking about me and our little talks together, the time we've spent with each other. She's not wasting anytime feeling bad about my broken heart, about betraying me and breaking all the little promises we made to each other. She's not remembering back to our walks home and our conversations, or even the silences. She does not taste the remnants of grape soda on her lips. She does not think of me.

I hope Tommy breaks her heart.

# RAIN DELAY

I am empty. July was my Christmas, all spangly and lit, with joy and birth and surprise gifts. Now it is over, ended with Linda's kiss, her betrayal, her lie. She has stripped all the ornaments from my tree, the tinsel, the garland, unstrung the lights, put them out, away. What's left is just the dead, bare skeleton, out on the curb with the barrel, waiting for the trash truck, oblivion.

Even my little baseball game, managing the old Pittsburgh Pirates, does nothing to give me reprieve from my sadness, despair, and hopelessness.

It is not 1966 as I pretend in my little made up game. It is 1977. The sad summer. I'm just a child playing with toys on the floor in my little bedroom. Foolish.

I turn over a card. Matty Alou, the speedy leadoff hitter slaps a single against Dodger great Sandy Koufax, pitching in what would be the hall of famer's last season, his elbow too painful, though his arm still firing strikes past the game's greatest hitters. How sad to be taken away from your calling at the height of your powers.

But my Pirates can't show sympathy. Our job is to beat Koufax and the Dodgers. The next card is flipped and steady shortstop Gene Alley moves Alou over to second with a sacrifice bunt. Next up is the great Roberto Clemente, but before he can step into the batter's box against Koufax, there is a rain delay.

I think of Clemente, killed in in a plane crash trying to help earthquake victims, a victim now himself. I remember his old baseball card from 1969, the white shirt over black undersleeves, black letters rimmed in gold. His face is angular, proud and bronze, despite the name written across the bottom of his picture, Bob Clemente. He was always criticized as a lazy Latin even though he went full out, elbows and knees flailing wildly as he ran. And though he could catch balls in the outfield while falling over backward, rolling over his neck and head and landing in a sitting position, as I saw diagramed with four pictures in one of my baseball guides. And what must be the worst thing for anyone, robbing him of his real name, calling him Bob though he was born Roberto, an American, in Puerto Rico. I learned all this from baseball and social studies, my two favorite subjects. Now the great Clemente is dead in his grave.

I splay across my bed, in tears, not for Roberto, for me.

I will never speak to Linda again. She is not who I thought she was, who she said she was. Thank you for not kissing me, she said. What a joke. Now she's making out with Tommy. I'll never make fun of you, she promised. No, you'll just humiliate me in front of everyone, betray me, take away everything that I thought I had and then laugh in my face like nothing ever happened.

What a set up. I should have known better.

She could call me if she wants to talk about it, to apologize. She could call me, but she doesn't. She doesn't care. How can she say she's sorry, if she's not sorry? I wouldn't believe her anyway.

I should just go over there, knock on her door, or shoot baskets and wait for her to come out. See if she has the guts. Then just say it to her, 'You're a liar. Everything you ever said to me was a lie. Tommy's stupid, huh? How stupid are you for kissing him, letting him put his tongue down your throat? How did it taste, huh?' That's what I should do. Tell her to her face, make her know she broke my heart.

Most of the time I'm up here in my room, crying, having conversations with myself. Deciding, not deciding. Avoiding my friends. Or laughing bitterly to myself, at myself, because even the top forty music charts are against me. The radio seems to alternate between Andrew Gold's "Oh, What A Lonely Boy," and America's new number one song, "I Just Want To Be Your Everything" by Andy Gibb. It takes the wind from my lungs every time. It kills me.

My mother habitually asks me if I want to go food shopping with her or do errands. I always say no, but this week I'm saying yes. It gets me out of my house, away from my friends.

One time this week my mother and I were wandering around Kmart and I saw Ant's old girlfriend Jenny, my first kiss, working behind the Icee counter. It made me feel good to think that someone else was as broken hearted as I was. I wanted to go up to her and say hello, tell her that I understood what she was going through.

She really is very pretty, I thought to myself, as I stood around the clothes racks deciding if I should go up and talk to her. The scent of lilac drifted somehow through my mind, there but not there. My lips tingled faintly at the remembrance of her kiss. Her blond hair surrounded her face in soft, golden light. How is it that a girl like her could like you and it wouldn't be enough?

For the first time since Vincent Beach I was thinking about someone else's problems. I felt sorry for Jenny. She deserved better than an asshole like Ant. I said her name in my mind. Maybe she would be happy to see me. Maybe I could help her.

A tall, muscley boy with a ponytail stepped up to her counter. He looked eighteen or more, and soon he had her laughing and flirting. Their faces leaned so close together it appeared at any moment they would kiss.

I didn't go over to say hello. She probably wouldn't remember me anyway, just some little kid shopping with his mother. That's probably what Linda saw, too. That's what everyone sees.


Whatever I can do to avoid my friends' calls, I do. I just can't be around Linda or Tommy. I can't be around anybody that was at Vincent Beach that day and pretend that everything is okay. It's not okay. I'm not okay and I want to be by myself. If I'm not out with Mom, I'm wandering through the reeds in the big field near the river, talking to myself, resolving, dissolving.

If I can just get through the next couple weeks, school will be starting and I can get back to my other friends, do other things, meet other girls, new girls. I'll be in high school then. Linda won't even be in my school.

But September is still a few weeks away and it feels rainy inside my head. On this August night, my baseball heroes are spread idly on the floor, my little index cards with their statistics gathering dust beside them.

The great Clemente is dead
Game called on account of rain.

# AUGUST COLLAPSE

It is late morning Friday, my first week in exile has nearly past, and I'm walking down Clifton to get to my reedy field where I can get lost and continue my private conversations with myself. Today I wonder if this was Linda's long range plot to get back at me for the trances, for feeling her and everybody else up, for not protecting her from that. Maybe I deserve this, to see her and Tommy making out high on a rollercoaster, a place I can't go.

This is how all my days are now, back and forth, new theories rising and falling across my heart. The army of hope marches in, the forces of despair beat it back, decimate it.

"Hey, invisible man!" I hear shouted from behind me. I keep going, pretending not to hear, hoping, as always, that pretending will be enough.

"Petey! Invisible man!" Rosie continues shouting.

I turn and he is nearly upon me.

"Hey, where have you been? It's like you disappeared," he says.

"I'm trying to," I say. I would vanish completely if I could and reappear on the first day of school.

"Why? I'm the one that should go into hiding," Rosie states, catching up with me. He lowers his voice. "You know Dawn is going out with Tommy now, don't you?"

"Oh, no man. I'm sorry," I say, but inside I am budding. I don't feel his disappointment. At least Tommy was telling the truth. He really did want to go out with Dawn, not Linda. I hope Linda is crushed. Let her feel what I feel.

"Tommy's like a serial killer," I continue. "First me, then you."

"Nah. It's not Tommy's fault. Dawn just likes him more than she likes me."

"That's what Tommy said."

"So you talked to him about it?" Rosie says. Little lines erupt on his forehead. I can see he doesn't like the idea of Tommy and me discussing his heartache. Things are bad enough without being a conversation topic.

"Just on the walk home from Burke's."

"When," he spits.

"The day we all went to Vincent Beach."

"Oh, that's nice. You two have a nice chat talking about me getting rejected? You must have had a good time laughing at me?"

"No, Rosie. Really I just didn't want to talk about what Linda did to me."

"What did she do to you?" he asks, a ripple of smile lights his eyes. He's happy that I'm hurt.

"You know what she did," I say. Again it seems like everyone wants to make me say it. I don't want to say it. I don't want to talk about it.

"No. I thought you guys were cool. In fact, I've been jealous of you and how much time you've been spending with her. It seems really good. That's what I wanted with Dawn."

"Well, you don't have to be jealous anymore," I say.

"Why? What happened?" His big wide-open freckly face almost convinces me he doesn't know, but he has to. He was right there.

"C'mon Rosie. You know. She made out with Tommy on the rollercoaster."

"Oh, that?" he says, his hand dismisses the thought with a wave of air. "No, he kissed her and she pushed him off, just like Dawn did to me. They weren't making out."

"That's not what Tommy said."

"Tommy? He's full of shit. What would you think he'd say anyway? 'I kissed Linda and she didn't like it'?"

"That's what you're saying about Dawn?"

"Yeah, but I'm not Tommy. Besides, everyone already knows anyway."

We walk on silently, letting things rest. Me, I'm lost wondering what really happened on the rollercoaster. Which version is true? Tommy's? Rosie's? And, what did my eyes really see? Can it really not be as much of a big deal as it felt to me at the time? Linda didn't seem ashamed or distant from me when she came up to me after. She started right in describing the ride to me. She even nudged me on the shoulder when Andy Gibb came on. Me, and only me.

Poor Rosie. He really is heartbroken. He has to watch his girl, the one he wishes was his girl, dating one of his best friends. It's not fair. Rosie's such a good guy. He was the first one of us to see the good in Dawn, to give her a chance to show us her good side. And she fell for Tommy who shitted on her the most. I guess it doesn't pay to be a nice guy. I should know that by now.

"It sucks about Dawn and Tommy," I say truthfully, thinking about someone else instead of myself for the first time all week. Well, except for those few moments at Kmart when I saw Jenny.

"Yeah, it does suck, but I took my shot." Yes, he did. That's what I should have done. Maybe things would be different now. I could have asked Linda out at the fireworks, or on her front step, or walking back from Chillwells, or through her window screen. Howard.

"What happened when you kissed her?" I ask.

"She fuckin' pinched my arm so hard I had to stop," he smiles, sadly. "I should have known she wouldn't like me doing that."

"What did she say to you?"

"Nothing then, but later on, after Vincent Beach, she came over to hang out with Karen and she asked to talk to me about it."

"What did she say?" I prod some more.

"She was real nice about it. She said she thought I was a nice guy, but that she just liked Tommy, and she said I shouldn't just be grabbing girls and kissing them. I said something stupid like 'Tommy did it, too,' and she just smiled at me, like a friendly smile, and just said that we've all done stupid things and that she was sorry it didn't work out, but that she thought plenty of girls liked me, but just not to be grabbing girls like I did to her. That's not right, she said."

"So what'd you say?"

"I said I'm sorry. I didn't know what to say. I was embarrassed. I just wanted to be by myself. It was like she was so mature and I was so immature. She even said she was sorry that my feelings were hurt. I mean, it still really sucks to see her with Tommy, but I still think she's nice. I mean, she was really nice about the whole thing."

"You were right about her," I say. "She's not so bad."

"I was so jealous of you dancing with her to that big band music. You two were nuts," he laughs.

"I tried to push you up there."

"I know. I know. But I'm no dancer."

We continue on down to the end of the street. My big reedy field is on the right, our old stone wall is on the left. Behind that, the grove of trees and the path that leads to the big Whyte fuel tank.

"A lot has happened down here this summer," Rosie says, standing up on the wall. "You know there's not going to be any drinking tonight. Tommy and Dawn are going to the movies with Burkie and my sister."

"That sucks," I say. "I mean I didn't feel like hanging out with those guys anyway, but the whole thing with Dawn and your sister out on a double date in Burkie's car. That sucks, Rosie."

"Yeah, it does. Dawn and Tommy have been together all week."

"I can't wait for school to start," I say.

"Me, neither," Rosie answers.

The summer heat hisses all around us. Insects hum busily in the trees.

"Hey, so did Linda really push Tommy away when he kissed her?"

"Yeah, what do you think?"

"Well, it didn't look like she pushed him away."

"What could you see from the ground? He's not going out with her, right?"

"I don't care about Tommy, Rosie, but don't bullshit me," I plead. "You were in front of them and you were kissing Dawn and all involved in that, how could you know how Linda reacted to Tommy's kiss?"

"Honest?"

"Yeah, of course," I demand.

"Honestly, I can't really say either way. I was just trying to make you feel better."

"Well, don't," I say. I'm in the desert. Don't hand me an empty glass and tell me it's full.

"Hey, you're still better off than me," he points out.

We let that sit for a few minutes, just hanging out on the wall, lost in our own thoughts.

"The Red Sox are really falling apart," I say to break the silence and change the subject.

"It's August," he replies. We're only teenagers, but we've lived through our share of Red Sox collapses. In 1972, Luis Aparicio, my hero and one of the greatest base runners of all time, fell down rounding third base with the tying run in the deciding game of the pennant race. In 1974, they entered September with a six game lead over the Baltimore Orioles and were out of it by mid-month. In 1976 they fell out of it early with a ten game losing streak. This year they killed the Yankees in June, but now it's another August collapse and 'wait 'til next year'.

The Red Sox did go to the World Series in 1975, losing to Cincinnati, the Big Red Machine, in seven games. Some called it the greatest World Series ever, but that's little consolation to the losers.

"I thought everything was gonna be great after seventy-five," I say. "With Lynn and Rice and Fisk, I thought sure they'd be at least winning the division every year. It seemed like the future was bright."

"Yeah, but you can't trust the future with them."

Yes, you can't trust the future.

"Hey, do you want to go down to the river and skim stones?" I ask Rosie.

"What? Are you seven?"

"It's something to do," I say defensively.

"Sure, let's go," he shrugs. We slip down off the wall and cross the street. We wander down through the tall reeds. The beginning is a winding, narrow path where the stalks grow tall over our heads. Gradually, the reeds get shorter and we can see the field of grass as the path opens and the river spreads out down below.

Suddenly, we here noises, voices, faintly. In the grass near the river, there is a couple, a boy and a girl lying with each other, making out. It is Tommy, on top of Dawn. Shaken, I turn to look at Rosie, but he has already spun around and began rushing back up the path. I follow behind him trying to keep up.

"I'm going home, Petey," Rosie says over his shoulder as we leaves the reeds and enter back onto the cracked, broken tar at the end of Clifton. Rosie does not look back. I follow behind him for a few steps, but there is nothing for me to say. He's now the invisible man, gone.

I stand still in the middle of this dead end street. I can't stay here long. Eventually Tommy and Dawn will come winding out of that path, laughing arm and arm, or just solemn in their shared intensity. I don't want to see them. I could go the other way, over the wall and through the grove of woods, out into the opening by the Whyte Fuel tank. There I could hang around in it's shadow and feel sorrow for myself, for Rosie. Have my little conversations. Try to figure things out.

Instead, I do the slow walk home. I feel now like Tommy and Dawn could come out of anywhere, be anywhere. Or maybe Burkie and Karen. I want to hide in my room and hope no one calls until after Labor Day comes. Then just run out to the bus with my notebooks on the first day of school.

# #*&%ING DAWN

Tommy has called me on the phone twice this morning, and now he is standing in my driveway. Why would I want to talk to him?

"Pe-ter!" he hollers in our two-syllable neighborhood call. That seems to be the only little kid thing left that he still does. Me, I'm up in my room playing pretend games and looking at my baseball cards. Those guys - Aaron, Mays, Willie Stargell, Yaz, Jim Rice – they're the only friends I want to see right now.

Still, Tommy stands and calls. My mother yells up the stairs as if I'm deaf. "Peter! Tommy's out front calling for you!"

It's Thursday, almost a week since Rosie and I stumbled across Tommy and Dawn down by the river, almost two weeks from the kiss at Vincent Beach.

"Hey Tom," I say, coming out my door. At least he doesn't have his basketball. I definitely don't want to go over to Linda's and shoot. I only need to keep my hideout plan going for another two and a half weeks and I'll be back in school, alive again.

"Hey Petey. Look, George took my basketball to play with his friends, so why don't you get yours and we can go shoot some?"

"I don't feel like shooting hoops," I say. I don't feel like doing anything out here in the light where people can see me, question me. I want to hide.

"Speaking of shooting," he grins. It's the same smile from our walk home from Burkie's after Vincent Beach, the smile I've wanted to punch off his face a hundred times.

"What?" I'm not playing his game.

"What me? What you? What have you been doing for two weeks? Nobody's seen you. It's like you're a ghost."

"I just don't feel like hanging out," I say. I am a ghost.

"It's not still the Linda thing, is it?" he asks.

I don't answer.

"The Linda thing. I didn't even want to do it. Rosie talked me into it. He wanted to kiss Dawn, but he wanted us all to kiss so he'd have some kind of excuse if Dawn didn't like it."

"Yah, sure. Blame Rosie." He can't even keep his story straight. Before it was 'I had my tongue down her throat'. Now, it's 'Rosie made me do it'.

"Look, I liked it. Linda's got nice lips. But I wanted Dawn and now I got her."

"Good for you," I pout. "So why'd you kiss Linda?

"I just told you. It was Rosie's plan. He wanted to kiss Dawn."

"But you liked Dawn, so why'd you let Rosie kiss her?"

"I didn't let him. He was going to kiss her either way. He said he liked her, so I had to let him have a chance."

"Besides, you knew she liked you anyway."

"That's right," he grins. There's that smile again. "Plus, when else was I gonna get a free shot at Linda?"

"You suck," I spit.

"I'm just kidding ya'" he tells me with a punch to the shoulder. "First it was fuck you, now I suck? Jeez. You can still take a shot with Linda."

"Did she push you away?" I ask.

"Nobody pushes Tommy away," he cracks, grin wide.

I'll fuckin' push you away, I think. I'm glad Linda wanted it from him. How does she feel now that he's making out with Dawn?

"So what did you do last night?" Tommy asks me.

"Nothing much," I shrug. He probably wouldn't be interested in the details of the little pretend baseball game I played last night. The 1966 Pirates handled their cross-state rivals, the Philadelphia Phillies, 8-3. Big Bob Veale, the hard throwing strikeout artist, got the victory.

"You want to know what I did last night?" He's on his toes, teeth shining.

"What?" I don't want to know.

"I fucked Dawn." He pounds his right fist into his left palm, just like a shortstop. Big smile.

"Yeah," I say with as little energy as possible. I do my best to hide my shock and anger, my jealousy really. I don't want any of that to leak out of my mouth or show in my eyes, but he's just shoveling shit into my face.

"She has this thing about being doubted, so I started on her. I said 'I doubt you like me that much', you know. Then I said 'I doubt you'd take your clothes off for me.' I said 'You act all adult, but you're not gonna do anything about it.'"

I'm asking no questions, trying to act as uninterested as possible, unaffected. I didn't ask to hear this story.

"Her bra was already off and, like her pants were unsnapped because I was fingering her, and she just took everything off." Part of me is picturing Dawn's pale nakedness, another bigger part is hating Tommy.

"So she was lying on her clothes in the grass, her bush out and everything, and I just took my dick out and I was like teasing her with it, and she just said 'Still doubt me?,' you know, all serious and everything, and I said yes." His eyes are wide searching me for some reaction.

"And she just said 'I told you not to doubt me' and pulled me on top of her. I still didn't think she'd do it, but she let me put it right in her. I didn't want to cum inside her, but I couldn't help. After a while it just bursts out," he marvels.

"What if she gets pregnant?" I ask, finally finding some kind of rain for his parade.

"She won't get pregnant just once," he says. "I stole some rubbers from George, so next time I'll be safe."

"She could already be pregnant, Tommy," I say, as if I know anything about it.

"Oh, you're just jealous," he says. "I'm going over to tell Burkie."

He's wrong. I'm not just jealous. I'm also sad, angry and scared. What is happening to me, to the world, to summertime? Where did it all go? Why did everything go wrong? And why did it have to change so fast? Everybody growing up, and me still this little boy lost in the wilderness, not prepared. Not prepared at all.

I thought at least Linda understood, but no more. And Tommy blaming the kiss on Rosie. I bet it was completely Tommy's idea. I bet he wanted to embarrass Rosie and humiliate me, all in one rollercoaster ride. I bet he had it all planned. And if Linda wanted to push him away she could have. She could have stopped him from kissing her at all. But I saw it. I saw them on that ride. She was kissing him.

Now he's got Dawn, I think to myself. Just when she seemed to be a good kid, doing those crazy dances with me at Vincent Beach. Now Tommy's wrecked her.

My impulse is just to burst apart at the seams, run in every direction, away from me.

Somehow something else inside of me rises up, makes a decision. I go back inside my house and get my basketball. Tommy's now way out of sight, having already crossed Winthrop. I walk further up the main road, past Elm, and take the next street, Porter, where I walk seriously for two blocks and then turn onto Ford.

I'm going to walk right up to Linda's door and just knock. I want to see her face when she finds out about Tommy and Dawn.

I drop my ball and begin dribbling deliberately as I approach Linda's house. I can't even look towards her house.

Instead I get in range of the hoop across the street and take my first shot. It clangs. I chase down the rebound and roll in for a lay-up, all the while trying to avoid looking behind me at Linda's house, at our old brick front step, at the door behind it.

I shoot again and again. Some good, some awful. My heart's not really in it. I'm stupid for even being here, a stupid little kid.

Clang. I hear a screen door bang behind me. This is what I wanted and what I was afraid of.

"Hey Petey!" It's Linda's cheerful voice, a sound that was once music to me. Still is. The sound of her makes something inside of me soften. I'm afraid if I turn around I'll collapse at her feet.

"Petey," I hear, coming closer. "Where have you been lately?"

I turn around and she is right upon me. The heat rages beneath my forehead. Her eyes are bright and so close.

"Hey," she smiles, her hair falling golden over her forehead. I am water. I have to catch my breath. I should just let everything go, but I can't. I don't.

"Why did you kiss him?" I spit. It takes the sunniness from her eyes.

"What?" Her mouth opens, bewildered.

"Why did you kiss Tommy?" I shout in her face.

"I didn't kiss him. He kissed me!" she claims.

"Yah, right. I saw you!" I wave an arm at her in disgust.

"I pushed him away as soon as I could," she pleads. She raises her hands toward my shoulders.

"He fucked Dawn!" I shout in her face. Her mouth falls open. It does hurt her. Good. See how I feel!

"Petey!" she says as I spin around and walk off, basketball under my arm. I cut back onto Porter and run as fast as I can. I run down Winthrop and across it, into my neighborhood. I run all the way to the end of Clifton, to the old stone wall. I climb over it and run through the woods and out to the clearing, to the big tank at Whyte Fuel.

If she liked me she would have chased me. She didn't even try to catch me. She likes Tommy. Now she knows how it feels.

I take my basketball and hold it like a baseball, rear my arm back and whip it as hard as I can at that stupid tank and listen to the loud wang it makes as it bounces off and dribbles itself against the ground below. When it stops I gather it into my arms and hug it to my chest like something lost. Then I collapse myself into a little ball on the ground and explode into sobs.

# THE KING IS DEAD

I sit for a long time after my sobbing stops, gathering my breath. The fuel tank stands in the distance like everything, distant from me. I don't really care about ever getting to the top of that tank no matter what Tommy or anyone else calls me. The problem is that everything I do want seems as far away and as impossible to get to as the top of that tank.

And, what do I really want anyway? Linda, I thought. Still think, somehow. But she doesn't want me. Why would she? I act more like a nine year old than fourteen. Or maybe five or six, some age before seven, the age of reason. I must have missed that one. On top of everything, I just screamed in her face and ran away from her, didn't even give her a chance to explain.

Still, she did the same thing. She ran away from those trances. She thought she was the baby. That look on her face, though, when I told her about Tommy and Dawn, that look I can't forget. She definitely likes Tommy. She liked the kiss.

Car doors thwack in the distance, from Clifton I think. There is a clatter of voices now. I stand and gather my self, basketball under arm. I think I hear Burkie's voice. God, I hope it's not him and Karen coming here for a make-out session, or maybe they're screwing now, too.

Why am I here with a basketball? What can I tell them? Someone stole my ball and I just found it down here?

Yeah, right. I was going to shoot baskets, but changed my mind after I left the house? Maybe.

"Hey, Petey. What are you doing here?" Burkie asks as he strides out of the wooded path. Ant follows right behind him.

"Hi guys," I muster. Why am I here with a basketball?

"What did you bring a basketball down here for?" Burkie grins at me.

"I don't know." Stupid, little kid answer.

Burkie shakes his head. Through a wide grin he says, "Fuckin' nut."

"I think you better go home," Ant says like he means it. Maybe he's mad about Jenny kissing me, even though I know she really was just making fun of me.

"I don't have to go home."

"You do if I tell you to."

"Aw, leave him alone, Ant. He's alright," Burkie says.

"Can you keep your mouth shut?" Ant asks me, eyes right on my eyes. "Can he keep his mouth shut, Burke?"

"Yuh," Burke answers first. "You won't say nothing, right Petey."

"Nothing about what?"

"He's a good kid, Ant. We've been drinking with him all summer and no one's got caught, so Petey can keep a secret."

"Alright," Ant nods. "I'm going on you, Burke." He pulls a pack of Marlborough cigarettes from his back pocket and flips open the lid. "But if this gets out I'm going to come for you, Petey. Understand."

"Yuh."

Ant hands a cigarette to Burke.

"Decent," Burke grins.

"You smoke?" I ask him.

"It's a joint, dickhead," Ant shoots.

This is different from drinking. Everybody drinks. My parents drink. All the parents drink. This is drugs.

I look up at Burke. "You smoke pot?"

He pulls a cigarette lighter from his pocket. "These things are good for more than just putting girls in trances," he says, flicking up the flame and touching it to the end of the joint.

He sucks in deeply from it, different from how people smoke cigarettes, and hands it over to Ant. They pass it back and forth to each other.

"You won't buy for us because your father's a cop, but you take drugs?" I say to Ant.

"I'm gonna beat you senseless!" he says, faking a punch at me that comes so close I throw my hands in front of my face. They explode in laughter.

"Where just getting high, Flinch," Ant shrugs.

"Flinch," Burkie giggles, pointing at me. "Good one. Hey, remember the one you said about him and the pussy, Ant? How he couldn't recognize it."

"I said he could recognize it. He'd be able to pick a pussy out of a lineup because it would be the one thing he'd never seen." They both burst into giggles.

"The one thing he'd NEVER seen!" Explosions of laughter.

"Hey, Ant. Can we let Petey have a toke?"

"I don't want to."

"It's not up to you," Ant says, taking the joint from Burke's fingers. "You have to take a toke, Flinch. Then you can't tell, cos you'll be guilty, too."

"I won't tell."

"That's right you won't." He touches the joint to my lips.

"Just suck in," Burkie says, fatherly. "Nothing's going to happen to you."

"Suck in."

I do as I'm told, too deeply. My throat burns smokey and bursts out forward into choking coughs. Burke and Ant giggle at me hysterically.

"Give me that thing!" Ant sputters and chuckles.

I finally regain my breath and say, "That's enough for me."

"I guess!" Burkie cries as the laughs tumble out of both of them.

"Get this," Ant says, mostly to Burkie. "I call over to Kelly's house," That's his new girlfriend with the dark hair and the tits leaping out of her shirt. "And she says, 'have you heard? Elvis Presley died.' And I'm like, yuh, so? So, she gets all bent out of shape, yelling at me like it's my fault or something. 'Oh my God, I can't talk to you!' she yells, bursts into tears and slams the fuckin' phone down."

"She hung up on you?" Burke is shocked.

"Elvis Presley died? What happened?" I ask. Am I getting high?

"Yah, she did. I mean what's she crying about anyway?" Ant asks. "She acts like her father croaked or something."

"Elvis Presley. That's old people's music anyway," Burkie says.

"Yeah, I mean Fonzie's probably pretty sad," Ant agrees. Fonzie's the cool, tough kid on "Happy Days," the most popular show on television. He's the Ant, I guess.

"The King is dead," Burke intones with his best Elvis impression.

"No more happy days for him," Ant replies.

"How did he die anyway?" I ask. If the King can die, can't we all? Won't we all? Am I just getting high? I can't get high from just one toke, can I?

"The fat fuck had a heart attack," Ant laughs. "Imagine that. He's the King. He can still get all the chicks he wants. He's got tons of dough, and he croaks at 42."

Was that even a toke that I had? I don't feel any different, I don't think.

"Did you ever end up calling Kelly back?" Burke wonders.

"Nah, fuck her," Ant dismisses, while his hand slices a wave through the air in front of him. "I ain't calling her back. She wants to cry over some dead guy she never even met, let her."

"That's right," Burkie answers.

"Besides, you know that waitress, Nancy, down at Papa Gino's?"

"Yuh, the Italian looking girl," Burke answers.

"That's right. She's Italian. She's also next."

I don't understand Ant or the big grin on his face. He's thinking of dumping a very pretty girl because she's sad about Elvis Presley dying. This is after he dumped beautiful Jenny, my first kiss girl. Now he's on to some waitress.

"Hey, why'd you break up with Jenny anyway?" I ask. I don't feel high. I don't feel different, like when we're drinking.

"Used up," Ant says. They both laugh.

"She was pretty. I saw her the other day at Kmart talking to some guy." I'm fine. I didn't have enough. They're high.

"If you were getting any pussy at all you'd know what I was talking about." More laughter. "You get bored with the same one after a while."

"You bored with Karen yet?" I say to Burke.

"Mind your own business, Flinch." He pounds my arm. I didn't have enough pot to not feel that.

"How's things going with your little girlfriend, Petey? What's her name?" Ant asks.

"Linda," I answer. It makes me feel big to say she's my girlfriend, but I know it's not true.

"Since when?" Burke bursts. "She's not his girlfriend. Flinch has never had a girlfriend."

"I didn't say she was my girlfriend. I just knew he was talking about Linda so I told him her name."

"Well, she looked like your girlfriend when I saw you at Chillwell's," Ant says. "She's gonna be sweet someday, you know? You better get on it now. A girl like that's never gonna put out, but what do you care? You wouldn't know what to do anyway?"

"You got that right," Burkie confirms, like he's ten years older than me. "But wait, Ant. He's already grabbed her tits. I told you about the trances. Remember?" More laughter.

"Give him the lighter, Burkie. He's gonna get this Linda girl in a trance."

"Yeah, take it, Petey. It's the only way she'll let you touch her." That's probably true now, too.

"Yuh, burnin' love! For the King!" Ant raves. They both start singing in deep exaggerated Elvis voices.

I'm done. I turn with my basketball tucked under my arm and head toward the path out. This stops there singing.

"Hey wait up, Petey. We'll give you a ride."

"I'm fine," I say. I don't need to be with these guys, or anybody, for one second longer. I want to run home, but I make myself walk. If I stay any longer the tears will just come, like a little kid.

"Well don't say nothin', Petey" Burkie shouts.

"Yeah, keep your mouth shut! I'll come for you, Petey. I swear!"

# WHAT ELSE?

What else is left to happen to me this summer? What else will be broken, taken away?

When I get through the woods and over the stone wall, I start running up Clifton just in case Ant and Burkie chase after me. When I get to the bend where the road turns and Tommy's house comes into view, I slow to a walk and continue.

Elvis Presley is dead. I remember a joke I got out of a Crackerjack box when I was younger. What's green and sings rock'n'roll? Elvis Parsley. I remember my mother smiling at that, but I didn't get it. It's a lousy joke even if you do get it. Crackerjacks are lousy, too. They're about the worst candy you can have, if they're even considered candy.

I don't even want to glance at Tommy's house as I go by. I just want to get past it and go home. I glance up at it anyway, on the hill. Then I look. I think I see Tommy and Dawn in the window, not looking out at me, looking at each other.

I run again.

Finally, I slope through the kitchen door of my house. My mom is stationed at the ironing board at work. The kitchen television is on, buzzing next to the refrigerator. "Did you here? Elvis Presley died."

"Yuh, I know." I won't to get through the kitchen as fast as I can. I don't want her to smell any pot on me.

"So young," she moans.

Before I can escape up the stairs to my room, she calls me back into the kitchen. Does she smell the pot? Can she tell I smoked? I edge back into the kitchen, half hiding behind a cabinet.

"Who were you shooting baskets with?

"Nobody."

"How come?"

Because Tommy's fucking Dawn, Burke and Ant are smoking pot, Rosie's heartbroken and Linda hates my guts.

"No reason."

"Why didn't you call somebody?"

"Didn't feel like it?"

"Were you hoping to see Linda?"

"Leave me alone!" I stomp up the stairs. I ran to get here and now I feel like running to get out. I want to just throw this basketball as hard as I can and keep throwing it.


It's about an hour later and I can here my father coming up the stairs. His steps always have a certain heaviness to them, like he's carrying something, or like he's going someplace he doesn't really want to go.

I hear his knuckles rap against the door.

"Dad?"

"Can I come in?"

"Yeah." I'm lying on my bed, where I've been since I put my basketball in the closet.

He comes in and stands by my feet. "Did ya hear about Elvis?"

"Yeah."

"I'm not much for rock'n'roll," he says. "But he was a good singer. He could really sing a good ballad. He was quite a dancer, too. Rock'n'roll dancing."

"Yeah." There is a long silence.

"You okay? Mom seems to think there's something bothering you."

"I knew she sent you up here."

"Your mother's just a little worried about you," he shrugs quietly. This is not what he wanted to be doing after a long day of work.

He turns and takes a couple steps toward my desk and picks up a piece of paper. "Who's Linda? This the girl from the other neighborhood, with the braids?"

"Oh my God. Leave me alone!" I flip over and bury my face in my arms.

"I just..." His voice trails off.

After a moment he begins again, "It'll be okay."

"What will? You don't have any idea what's going on. Just leave me alone," I shout into my bed.

A long moment later his heavy footsteps move toward the door. His hand touches my shoulder. "We'll call you down for dinner."

"Don't!"

# Dawn Comes

I never left my room last night, never left my bed. Didn't go down for supper or to watch TV. I've spent two weeks trying to hide from everybody and forget all about Linda, and now even my parents know. That stupid letter that I never wrote. Dear Linda. I should have torn up that piece of paper the night of the kiss. Instead I leave it on my desk for my mom to see while she's snooping around. I can't even leave my room now.

I go over to the window, but it's not what it used to be. It once was a place of wonder, where I would look out and imagine, past the glimmering, leafy trees, past the pulsing tar of the main street, beyond the roof tops of the next neighborhood, down old Ford Street to that brick step, that corner bedroom, that girl.

Gone.

As I look out the window now, it's just a place I can't be. Places I can't be. I can't go to Burkie's or Tommy's. They've got girlfriends now. I can't go to Rosie's. He's hiding like me. I definitely can't play hoops out in front of Linda's house.

Still, I watch out this window, watch and look as if something will somehow change.

Just now coming into view walking up Clifton Street is Dawn. She cuts along sharply, probably returning from another time with Tommy in the field by the river, black t-shirt, dungaree shorts, red sneakers, dark hair falling back behind her. I can't believe she let Tommy screw her. It seems like she wanted it as much as him. I don't understand any of it. We were all just walking around goofing on each other at the beginning of summer and now Burkie's driving, Tommy and Dawn are screwing, pot. The King is dead.

I step back from the window to a place where Dawn can't see me, but I can still see her walking along, past my house and over toward her apartment building down the other end of Carter. Except she doesn't pass my house. She comes right up the walk and begins rapping on my door.

I hear my mother open it below me and after a few words she's yelling up the stairs, "Petey, there's a young lady here to see you."

Now where do I go?

I trudge down the stairs, reluctant, angry. Dawn has wandered down to the end of the walk, waiting for me.

"I invited her inside, but she said she'd rather wait on the walk," my Mom says, as if that is the strangest thing that she's ever seen.

"Okay," is all of my answer.

I come out the door and Dawn smiles softly at me.

As I approach she reaches for my hand and says, "Come with me, Petey."

"Get the fuck away from me you fuckin' whore," I blurt.

Whack. I feel Dawn's right hand crack into my left cheek.

"That's just stupid and mean," she pronounces firmly. Her dark eyes, rimmed in blue liner, search my face. "If I even thought you could say something like that, I wouldn't be here."

"Why are you here?" I ask sharply.

"I came here because your making a mistake, and I want to help you fix it."

"I don't need your help," I pout. What kind of help can she give me anyway?

"Yah, you do. You really do. You're doing everything wrong," she says seriously. She might have something there. With a tap on my arm she gets me to start walking.

"So you're gonna tell me the right things to do?"

"Yah, Petey, I am. I think I know how you feel, and I know you like Linda. You're just taking everything wrong," she continues, really looking into my face from under her dark hair.

"I don't like Linda," I lie.

Dawns stops and stands right in front of me. She smiles and says, "Me and you are a lot alike."

"I'm nothing like you," I say, bitterly.

"Don't be like that," she says. "You were the only one of the guys who would dance with me at Vincent Beach, remember? The other guys wished they were you. I mean, who wouldn't want to dance with me?" She grins sunny and wide.

I smile. I can't help it.

"Yeah, but you did it. You weren't afraid of how we looked, or what everyone else would say."

"So?"

"So, you're a cool guy when you give yourself a chance. When you're not locked in your house."

"I just don't feel like hanging out."

"You're just scared and that's okay."

"I'm not scared. What are my scared of?" She doesn't know me. She's nothing like me.

"The same stuff I'm scared of," she says. She looks suddenly soft, a little kid like me.

"You're scared?"

"Of course, I'm scared. I moved into this neighborhood and you guys all knew each other and I didn't know anyone. I didn't know if I would fit in."

"That's what Rosie said, but you don't act scared. You're about as confident a girl as I've ever met."

"I act confident because I'm scared. It's just an act to help me fit in, to get kids to think they should fit in with me," she says, looking into my face.

"Why are you telling me this?"

"Cos there's more reasons I'm scared, reasons you're scared, too. We both know that there's a lot more to the world than our little lives now, our little neighborhood, something better. And you're scared that you're never gonna get there, that you don't know how to get there."

She's right, but I don't know how to say it, to accept it.

"See," she says, her blue-rimmed eyes training right on mine. "I know how you feel cos I feel it, too."

"We're not going to Tommy's are we?" I ask, still suspicious that this is all part of a grand plot to humiliate me, utterly.

"No, we're just walking," she says.

We keep going, past Tommy's and on.

"I just don't know who to trust," I confess.

"Hey," she lights up. "You trusted me enough to dance with me at Vincent Beach and we had a blast!"

"Yeah, you're a good dancer."

"You, too, Petey. That's what I'm telling you. You've got to be that kid that dances. You can't stand on the side like you've been doing the last couple weeks. Nothing happens to wallflowers."

"I don't know. Things have just sucked lately."

"I know they have, Petey. But you're being too hard on yourself. And you're being way too hard on Linda."

"You think so?" I ask, hoping she can convince me. Maybe this isn't some kind of trick.

"I don't know everything, but I do know that you have to talk to Linda," Dawn says.

"Why do I need to do anything?"

"That's another way you're like me," she says. "We both say mean things to hide our wonderfulness."

"Now I know why Rosie likes you."

Dawn nods, "He saw through my act."

"Tommy, too," I say.

"No," she smiles. "Tommy likes my act."

We're almost at the bend on Clifton. If we keep walking we'll be able to see the old rock wall, the trees, and beyond that, the Whyte Fuel tank.

"You really think I should talk to Linda?"

"You'll feel miserable until you do. And she didn't do anything wrong."

She's right, probably about everything. I am miserable, that's for sure.

"Linda's down on the rock wall waiting for you. Go and talk to her."

"You planned all this," I say.

"Yup. That's what friends are for," she smiles. She puts both her hands on my head, just like at Vincent Beach after our dance, and kisses me on the forehead. She turns away and starts walking back up Clifton.

"Hey Dawn," I call, rushing up behind her, overcome with a feeling for her, a tenderness. As she turns back to me, I just say it. "Please, don't get pregnant."

She wraps her arms around me in a warm, tight hug, saying nothing. It feels good. She let's me go and takes a couple backward steps, softly smiling, and turns to walk away.

"Oh and Petey," she says, whipping her head around, black hair flying with it. "Come up with a better first line than the one you used with me."

# PINKIE SWEAR

Birds sing above me in the trees, a fruity little warble, wafting in and out of the warm breeze. The sun is warm against my face, my arms. I watch for as long as I can, Dawn striding away from me and turning up the hill toward Tommy's house. I watch until she disappears.

She has left me with something. But do I trust it?

It is just me now, alone, with a choice to make. Here at the bend of Clifton, I must decide how the rest of this summer will be, what it will mean. At one end is my room and my baseball cards and my plan to remain in hiding until the school year starts. Safety. At the other end is a girl, the girl, and a hard conversation that I can't predict or control.

Part of me, inside, is already running up Clifton for home, for hiding. Part of me is thinking about the girl that whispered to me through her window screen. That seems so long ago, so long gone. But she is just steps away, down at the end of the street. Could she really want to talk to me? The birds are going to continue singing either way.

A seam opens in my stomach. I'm being controlled here, forced into forgetting my own feelings, manipulated. Why should I talk to Linda? She lied to me. She always said Tommy was stupid, then she ends up making out with him. I know what I saw on that rollercoaster. I know the look she had on her face when I told her about Dawn and

Tommy. She lied. She likes him and she always said he was stupid.

How could she do this to me, break all our little promises? She seemed so sweet, so different from everybody else. Turns out she's just the same. On top of everything, she's a liar, an actress. It was all an act.

The heat rises inside my chest, flowing up to my forehead. I'm gonna tell her. I'm gonna make her admit she's a liar and a fake. Then I can go home to my room and know it's just two weeks to a new start, a new life, maybe a new girl to think about. There's gonna be plenty of girls in high school and she's not gonna be one of them. She'll be back in eighth grade. Why should I worry about a junior high schooler?

I start walking toward the dead end of Clifton, where Linda supposedly waits. Maybe she's not even there. Maybe it's just another lie, a trick to embarrass me further.

I round the bend and my breath catches. I need to gasp and gulp a little air as I try to control my breathing. Linda is there, sitting on the old, rock wall, shorts and sneakers, red t-shirt, her sandy hair split into two long braids. My gosh. I want to just melt, fall at her feet in a little pile of forgiveness, or even apology. It takes an effort to walk seriously, briskly. I consciously firm up my jaw, my expression. She needs to answer.

She lifts her right arm and gives me a little bent hand wave. I consciously stop myself from acknowledging it, from answering with a sunny little kid wave of my own arm.

As I get closer she squints up at me, into the sun, and says, "I miss you."

I miss you, too, almost rushes from my mouth, but I stop it, force it back down. She's not going to get off that easy. "Why did you kiss him?" I ask, my teeth gritting.

"He kissed me, Petey," Linda says, her palms upturned in front of her. "I pushed him off as soon as I could."

"Yeah, right. I saw what I saw,"

"He hardly even touched me," she claims.

"That's not what he said. He said he had his tongue down your throat."

"Oh, he's stupid. He's just bragging. He even apologized to me after," she says.

"Sure, figures you'd stick up for Tommy." The responses just run from my mouth, unchecked.

"I'm not sticking up for him. He told me he was sorry for doing it, that it was all Rosie's idea, because he wanted to kiss Dawn."

"Oh, you just like him. That's all. I saw the look on your face when I told you about him and Dawn. Your jaw almost dropped off your face," I push.

"Yuh! Not 'cos of Tommy and Dawn. Because they went all the way!"

"You just wish it was with you," I spit.

"You're being so mean and you've got no reason to be. I didn't do anything wrong. And what if I did? What if I really did do something wrong? You can't even forgive me for nothing, for something that wasn't even my fault."

"So you admit that you were wrong," I continue, stupid.

"No, I wasn't wrong! He kissed me and I pushed him off. I'm just saying, I forgave you and you won't even give me a break when it wasn't even my fault."

"Forgave me! Forgave me for what?"

"For feeling me up," she says, quietly

Oh, for that.

"Yeah," I stop in my tracks. "I'm really sorry for that. I don't even know why I did it. I wasn't gonna."

"I thought you would protect me from the other guys."

"That's what I wanted to do, that's what I did do, but then something just came over me."

"That's what Dawn said was gonna happen. She said 'no boy can resist a free shot.'"

There is nothing to say.

"I was so mad at you when you felt up Dawn and Karen during that other trance, but I didn't think you'd do it to me."

"I know. I'm such a jerk. It made me feel like I was just like Tommy," I confess.

"You're not like him. At least you don't want to be. That's why I forgave you. I know you better than that," she says.

"You never even said anything to me about it," I recall.

"That's cos I forgave you," she say, palms up like evidence.

It was all my fault. Everything. But not the kiss.

"Did you forgive Tommy for kissing you like that?"

"Yeah, he said he was sorry. I'm not gonna hold a grudge against him for it. We're all friends."

"Your right, Linda. I'm sorry. I should've just trusted you," I say, looking down at my feet. "It just hurt to think of you kissing Tommy. I mean, whenever we're together it feels different from when I'm with anybody else. It just feels realer, you know?" I lift my head to look at her.

She nods her head a couple times. "Yuh."

The birds sing, I notice. They have probably been singing all along, but now I notice.

"Remember one night you said to me you believe every word that I say?" She squints up at me.

"Yeah," I say, realizing that I should have remembered that all along. I should have just trusted her.

"It's because there's no pressure with you, you know. I feel like I can say anything to you and you'll understand, or try to. But this time you didn't even try to believe me. You expected the worst."

"I know. I do that. I'm always ready to be...I don't know."

"Disappointed," she finishes my sentence.

"Yeah."

"I think we're different from that, Petey. It feels different to me, but you gotta trust me."

"I do trust you. I just got mad, jealous," I admit.

She lets that hang for a while. She slips off the wall and stands right in front of me, looking into my eyes. "Petey, I'm not ready," she starts. "I'm not ready to be like Karen and Burke. And I'm definitely not ready to be like Dawn and Tommy."

"I know," I say, not knowing any other way to respond.

"You're not ready, either, I don't think," she says.

"I like you," I blurt.

"I know, me too. I liked you walking me home all those times this summer. It's been a really nice summer," she says quietly.

"Until I wrecked it," I admit. "I should have just trusted you."

"Come with me," she says and climbs up and over the wall. I follow as she jogs onto the path and through the grove of trees and out into the clearing by the big fuel tank.

"I did lie to you about something," she says.

"Really?" What's this now?

"Yuh, I'm not really afraid of heights. I just said so when Tommy was making fun of you for not climbing the tank. I figured it would make you feel better."

It did. It does. "I was wondering how you could ride that rollercoaster if you're afraid of heights. It's really high."

"Yuh, it is," she says. "So is that." Her eyebrows arch up. With her chin she motions over her shoulder to the big tank.

"Have you ever climbed it?" I ask.

"Yes. Me and Dawn were up there today before she went to get you."

"So you had a whole plan," I smile.

"Yes. I didn't think you were ever gonna talk to me the way things were going."

I just stand here, dumbly.

"So do you want to go up?" she smiles.

"Me?"

"Yuh. You and me."

"I'll try," I nod. We walk over to the base of the long staircase that spirals up around the tank. I'm vibrating like a struck gong. No one else could talk me into this. The thought goes through my head that this could be the final step in a huge plot, concocted by Linda, Dawn and Tommy, to get me to the top of the tank and then leave me there as Linda hurries back down the stairs, laughing.

Linda takes the first two steps and turns and looks back at me. "You ready," she says.

I nod and follow her up hesitantly, slowly.

"Don't look down," she says.

"That's impossible," I say. "Everybody says that."

Slowly she continues ahead of me. About a third of the way up I feel my hand trembling. There is a big coming apart inside me. Linda is five or six steps above me.

"You okay?" she says.

"I don't know." And I don't.

"Just look at me, okay?"

"Okay," I say and I do. Slowly and steadily she continues upward. I follow along watching the back of her legs, her left leg really, from the bottom of her shorts to the bottom of her calf. I watch that and hold steady to the railing as we go up and up. Waves of heat rush through my stomach and chest, my head, but I keep moving, keep my eyes on her leg, it's bending.

She steps onto the top of the tank and turns toward me. She takes my hand and I am up on top, too, on steady ground. We walk several steps in from the rim.

Linda puts her hands on my shoulders and smiles into my face, "You okay?"

"Yuh," I breathe deeply and then dissolve into giggles. "You're the only person on Earth that could get me to do this."

"Look," she says, turning and pointing. A few feet away there are two soda cans, grape. We bend down and open them up, raise them and clink them together.

"How'd you know I'd actually come up here?" I wonder aloud.

"I hoped," she smiles. "Come over here," she says, leading me across the tank.

"I don't want to go too close to the edge," I say.

"Me, neither," she says.

We stop four or five feet from the rim and take in the wide view. Way up on the hill to the left we can see the shopping mall in Taft. In front of us, the downtown steeples of three churches. To the left, the shoreline and the ocean out to the horizon.

"Thank you," I say.

She just looks out in front of us. Silence, except for the hum of cars in the streets in the distance, the rustle of the wind working through the leaves of the trees below.

"Are you looking forward to high school?" she asks.

"Kinda," I say. Before today it was all I was looking forward to. "Tommy says that every year the seniors hang a freshman about my size upside down by the ankles from the crossroads, but I don't believe him."

"Sounds like something he'd say," Linda says sitting down and pulling her knees close to her chest. "What's the crossroads, anyway?"

"I don't even know," I laugh.

176

"I wish we were still in the same school," she says.

"Me, too," I answer. "It'll only be for one year, though."

I lay back flat and look up at the huge blue sky.

She stretches out next to me. "Look at that wispy cloud. It's like a horses head," she says.

This is what I imagined after Linda talked to me through her window screen. This is what I thought about later that night in my bed, just laying next to Linda. I wasn't thinking about messing around or anything urgent. It was just peaceful, beautiful, her and I together, side by side in a field, talking, giggling. Just like this, I think. I want to tell her how awesome this feels, all my worries and anguish gone, how this is really just a dream come true for me.

"I dreamt about this," I say to her. "Well, I imagined it. The night after you brought me to your bedroom window. I just layed awake for a while trying to imagine being next to you."

"In bed?"

"No, not in bed, but like in a field, just talking." I continue looking straight up to the sky. "And now here we are and I just want to say, I don't know, just that it feels great. It always feels great when we're together."

Her eyes don't move, but the corner of her lip turns up. "You know what I was thinking about that night after you went home?" she asks.

"What?" I say softly.

She turns her face toward me and says, "I was thinking how cool it would be to sneak out my window and us just stay out all night long talking and walking around."

"That would be cool," I smile. I look at her face, her eyes, until it's too much and I have to look back to the sky. The silence purrs around us, folds over us like a blanket. Everything has changed. "I'm so sorry about being so mad at you. You didn't do anything wrong. Especially after the way I acted during the trances."

"It's okay," she says.

The blueness of the sky, the clouds, the hum of noise from below, our neighborhood, the whole world, it spins around us.

"I don't want to wreck this," I say. "You know, I'm gonna try not to." I turn and look at her. She is still looking toward me.

"Can we make a deal?" she asks.

"Yes," I nearly whisper. I will make any deal with her.

"If one of us does anything that messes things up, let's promise to just to fix it."

"I promise," I pledge. I promise.

She lifts her left hand up near my face, littlest finger extended out, her brow sets seriously over her eyes, "Pinkie swear?"

I wrap my smallest right finger around hers. "Pinkie swear."

We let our hands fall between us, little fingers entwined. We lie here together, connected, at the very top of the tank, the world.

On top of everything.

Special thank you to Richard Martin and Kato Mele, talented writers and generous friends, who read and commented on an early manuscript of this novel.

Extra special thank you to Kerry Zagarella who nursed, cajoled and edited this entire project, tirelessly giving of her time, talent and insight. Without her, this book would not exist.

Finally, to Jack Powers, Dr. Sydney Rosenthall and Kerry Brown – providers of opportunity, inspiration, belief and wisdom – throughout my education as a writer – in and out of the classroom.